Dedicated to Everybody —

but copyright reserved.

R C

RANDOLPH CALDECOTT TREASURY

Randolph Caldecott, 1879

THE
RANDOLPH CALDECOTT TREASURY

SELECTED AND EDITED BY ELIZABETH T. BILLINGTON

WITH AN APPRECIATION BY MAURICE SENDAK

FREDERICK WARNE

NEW YORK · LONDON

The jacket and title page illustrations are from *The Great Panjandrum Him-self*, published in 1885. On page I 'Sketching under Difficulties,' an illustration to *Breton Folk. A Tour in Artistic Brittany*, 1880. The dedication on page V is from *A Sketch-Book of R. Caldecott's*, 1883. The illustration on page VI appears in *Come Lasses and Lads*, 1884.

Frederick Warne & Co., Inc.
New York, New York

Printed in the United States of America
by A. Hoen & Co.
Separations by Dichroic Color Inc.
Composition by Frost Bros. Inc.
Binding by A. Horowitz & Son
Designed by Denise Schiff
Production by Nancy Cristy

Library of Congress Catalog Card Number: 76-45308
ISBN: 0-7232-6139-3

1 2 3 4 5 82 81 80 79 78

CONTENTS

PRODUCTION NOTE

Every effort has been made to obtain the best reproduction sources for this book. The majority of color
plates were made from the first woodblock renderings
of Caldecott's work, which are, in essence, the original
art. All of the prints from early editions of the *Picture
Books* are reproduced in their original size. Several
plates are of re-renderings of the woodblocks. In these
instances the art was not copied in its original size,
and we have made enlargements or reductions accord-
ingly. The sketches and drawings were gathered from
a variety of sources, including books and collections,
and are a true indication of Caldecott's hand, whereas
the color plates represent a coordinated effort between
Caldecott and his engraver.

Occasionally the reader will observe broken areas or
cracks in the color plates. These are caused by the
separation of the small pieces of boxwood which, held
together with tongues of wood and glue, form the large
boxwood blocks. They are a part of the character of
the prints themselves. Since much of Caldecott's line
work was rendered and reproduced in brown, we have
used the color throughout the book. In addition, our
paper was chosen so as to match as closely as possible
the color, feel, bulk, opacity, and printability of the
paper used for the original *Picture Books*.

In the preparation of a book such as this, the assist-
ance of many people is vital. Our thanks go to Bill
Weisler of Frost Brothers for the typography, Martin
Schwatt of Baldwin Paper, Len Snyder and Ed Snyder
of Dichroic for the color separations, Paul Mound of
A. Hoen for the printing, and Ken James and Bud
Beam of A. Horowitz & Son for the binding.

PREFACE

This book contains a representative collection of drawings by Randolph Caldecott. Included are many of his early drawings as well as his better-known work. However, the *Treasury* would never have come into being without the interest and help of many people on both sides of the Atlantic. It is impossible to list all the people, but special thanks go to Mr. C. W. Stephens of Frederick Warne & Co. of London, who first encouraged the idea. I am grateful to Mrs. Lynn Knight-Smith, who made me warmly welcome in Caldecott's old studio, which is now her home.

Thanks to fellow "Caldecotters" Isobel Wilner, Virginia Haviland, and Michael Hutchins, who shared the quest.

I am indebted to the librarians of Chester, Whitchurch, Manchester, the New York Public Library, the Westchester Library System, Westchester County, N.Y., The Free Public Library Association of St. Augustine, and the St. Augustine Historical Society of Florida.

Caldecott wished his personal life to be kept private. I hope that this work does not violate his wish and that, if he were alive, it would please him.

Portrait of Randolph Caldecott engraved on wood

RANDOLPH CALDECOTT: AN APPRECIATION

BY MAURICE SENDAK

If any name deserves to be permanently joined with that of Mother Goose, it is Randolph Caldecott. His picture books should be among the first volumes given to every child.

Early in 1878, Caldecott began his illustrations for some of the better-known nursery rhymes, and no artist since has matched his accomplishments in this genre. To me, his work heralds the beginning of the modern picture book. There is in Caldecott a juxtaposition of picture and word, a counterpoint that never happened before. Words are left out—but the picture says it. Pictures are left out—but the word says it. It is like a bouncing ball; it goes back and forth. In short, it is the invention of the picture book.

Basically, there are two approaches to illustrating these elusive rhymes, the first being the direct, no-nonsense approach that puts the facts of the case into simple, down-to-earth images: Miss Muffet, her tuffet, curds, whey, and spider, all clearly delineated so as to erase any possible confusions in the child's mind. The second is the way Caldecott chose. As in a song, where every shade and nuance of the poem is heightened and given greater meaning by the music, so Caldecott's pictures illuminate the rhymes. This is the *real* Mother Goose—marvelously imagined improvisations that playfully and rhythmically bounce off and around

the verses without ever incongruously straying. They have that kind of spontaneous, rushing quality which I identify with the picture book.

The word *quicken*, I think, best suggests the genuine spirit of Caldecott's animation, the breathing of life, the surging swing into action that I consider an essential quality in pictures for children's books. Sequential scenes that tell a story in pictures, as in the comic strip, are an example of one approach to animation. In terms of technique, it is no difficult matter for an artist merely to simulate action, but it is something else to *quicken*, to create an inner life that draws breath from the artist's deepest perception.

Happily, Caldecott was endowed with a fabulous sense of lively animation. Characters who leap across the page, loudly proclaiming their personal independence of the paper—this is perhaps the most charming feature of a Caldecott picture book. His illustrations for *The Queen of Hearts* are an instance of his extraordinary development of this new form. He takes off sedately enough by picturing his theme ("The Queen of Hearts, she made some tarts") simply and straightforwardly. Then begin the purely Caldecottian inventions, the variations that enrich and build the nursery rhyme into an uproar of elaborate and comical complications. He accomplishes this not with flowing drawings in sequence across each page, but with tremendously animated scenes that rush from page to page. The delightful crescendo reached at the line "And beat the Knave full sore" is worth describing: in the background Caldecott pictures the Knave being soundly trounced by the King to the rhythm of a minuet danced gracefully in the foreground by a lady and gentleman of the court.

The word *quicken* has another, more subjective association for me. It suggests something musical, something rhythmic and impulsive. It suggests a beat—a heartbeat, a musical beat, the beginning of a dance. To conceive musically for me means to quicken the life of the illustrated book. I've long felt that children respond most spontaneously to illustrations that have a sense of music and dance and are not something just glued onto the page. And since music is the impulse that most stimulates my own work, it is the quality I eagerly look for in the work of the picture-book artists I admire.

It is, of course, impossible to know whether Randolph Caldecott related his own work to music, but it is also impossible to imagine his not being conscious, at least to some extent, of his musical sympathies. His pictures abound in musical imagery; his characters are forever dancing and singing and playing instruments. More to the point is his refinement of a graphic counterpart to the musical form of theme and variations, his delightful compounding of a simple visual theme into a fantastically various interplay of images, his clever weaving in of black-and-white sequences of drawings that both amplify and enrich the color pictures.

I can't think of the work of Caldecott without thinking also of music and dance. No one in a Caldecott book ever stands still. If the characters are not dancing, they are itching to dance. They never walk; they skip. Almost the first we see of The Great Pan-

jandrum Himself is his foot, and its attitude makes us suspect that the rest of his hidden self is dancing a jig. And think of Caldecott's clowning Three Jovial Huntsmen, red in the face, tripping, sagging, blowing frantically on their horns, receding hilariously into the distance, and then galloping full blast back at you. The work has the vivacity of a silent movie, and the huntsmen are three perfect Charlie Chaplins. The book is a veritable song-and-dance fest with its syncopated back-and-forthing between words and pictures. It has a galloping, rhythmic beat that suggests a full musical score, and I am infatuated with this persistent musical accompaniment Caldecott provides in his books, for I have reached for that very quality in my own.

His *Hey Diddle Diddle* and *Baby Bunting*, too, exemplify the rhythmic syncopation between words and images—a syncopation that is both delightful and highly musical. In most versions of *Hey Diddle Diddle*, the cow literally jumps over the moon. But here, the cow is merely jumping: the moon is on the horizon in the background and, from this perspective, only gives the *appearance* of being under the cow. In this way, Caldecott is being exceedingly logical, since he obviously knows the cow can't jump over the moon. But within his logic he shows you, on the color page, two pigs dancing, the moon smiling, the hen and the rooster carrying on—all of it perfectly acceptable to him and to us. Yet Caldecott won't go beyond a certain "logical" point: the cow *seems* to be jumping over the moon, but in fact it's just leaping on the ground—and, still, this is bizarre enough to make the milkmaid drop her pail of milk.

Now there's a reason for her dumping over the milk, for when you turn the page to read "The Little Dog laughed to see such fun," you might well have taken this line as a reference to the cow's having jumped over the moon. It refers, however, to the spilt milk—or whatever was in that pail—now being gobbled up by the two pigs, while the cow stares from the corner watching it all happen, and the maid looks down, perplexed, perhaps annoyed. So Caldecott has interjected a whole new story element solely by means of the illustrations, adding and ramifying, like a theme and variations, on top of the line, image upon image.

And from this absurdity and silliness, you turn the page to find one of his greatest and most beautiful pictures—"And the Dish ran away with the Spoon," accompanied by a drawing of the happy couple, obviously in love. Then there is the shock of turning the page and finding a final picture of the dish broken into ten pieces—obviously dead—and the spoon being hustled away by her angry parents, a fork and a knife. There are no words to suggest such a close to the adventure; it is a purely Caldecottian invention. Apparently he could not resist enlarging the dimensions of this simple nursery rhyme by adding a last sorrowful touch. So it all ends tragically. The pounding, musical quality of the book culminates in this strange final note. And that's Caldecott: words taking on unobvious meanings, colors, and dramatic qualities. He *reads* into things, and this, of course, is what the illustrator's job is really about—to interpret the text much as a musical conductor interprets a score.

The situation in *Baby Bunting* is a bit more conventional: the baby's getting dressed, Father's going a-hunting, looking a little ridiculous as he disappears behind a wall, followed by that wonderful dog trotting after him. But Father's frantic hunting is ineffectual, and all comes to naught. So they rush off to town to buy a rabbit skin. And this, of course, is pure Caldecott: the father dressed in hunting regalia with his dog, unable to kill a rabbit, finally winding up in town to *buy* the skin.

Father brings the rabbit skin home to wrap the Baby Bunting in, and what follows is a scene of jollity: the baby dressed in that silly garment, everyone rushing around, pictures on the walls from other Caldecott picture books. Then there is the lovely illustration of Mama and Baby.

And now again, Caldecott does the unexpected. The rhyme ends ("To wrap the Baby Bunting in"), but as you turn the page you see Baby and Mother strolling—Baby dressed in that idiotic costume with the ears poking out of his head—and up on the little hillside a group of about nine rabbits playing. And the baby—I'd give anything to have the original drawing of that baby!—Baby is staring with the most perplexed look at those rabbits, as though with the dawning of knowledge that the lovely, cuddly, warm costume he's wrapped up in has *come* from those creatures. It's all in that baby's eye—just two lines, two mere dashes of the pen, but it's done so expertly that they absolutely express . . . well, anything you want to read into them. I read: astonishment, dismay at life—is this where rabbit skins come from? Does something have to die to dress me?

After the comedy of what has preceded, the last scene again strikes that poignant note. Caldecott is too careful and too elegant an artist to become melodramatic; he never forces an issue, he just touches it lightly. And you can't really say it's a tragedy, but something hurts. Like a shadow passing over quickly. It is this which gives a Caldecott book—however frothy its rhythms, verse, and pictures—an unexpected depth at any given point within the work, and its special value.

When I came to picture books, it was Randolph Caldecott who really put me where I wanted to be. Caldecott is an illustrator, he is a songwriter, he is a choreographer, he is a stage manager, he is a decorator, he is a theater person; he's superb, simply. He can take four lines of verse that have very little meaning in themselves and stretch them into a book that has tremendous meaning—not overloaded, no sentimentality in it. Everybody meets with a bad ending in *A Frog he would a-wooing go*. Frog gets eaten by a duck, which is very sad, and the story usually closes on that note. But in Caldecott's version, he introduces, oddly enough, a human family. They observe the tragedy much as a Greek chorus might—one can almost hear their comments.

In the last picture, we see only Frog's hat on a rock at the stream's edge, all that remains of him. And standing on the bank are a mother, father, and two children. It's startling for a moment, until you realize what Caldecott has done. It is as though the children have been watching a theatrical performance; they're very upset, obviously. There are no words—I'm just inventing what I think it all means: Frog is dead, it alarms them, and, for support, they are clinging to their parents. The older child, a girl, clutches her father's arm; the younger holds fast to his coat. The mother has a very quiet, resigned expression on her face. Very gently, she points with her parasol toward the stream and the hat. The father looks very sad. They're both conveying to the children, "Yes, it is sad, but such things do happen—that is the way the story ended, it can't be helped. But you have us. Hold on, everything is all right." And this is impressive in a simple rhyming book for children; it's extremely

beautiful. It's full of fun, it's full of beautiful drawings, and it's full of truth. And, frankly, Caldecott did it best, much better than anyone else who ever lived.

One can forever delight in the liveliness and physical ease of Caldecott's picture books, in his ingenious and playful elaborations on a given text. But so far as I am concerned, these enviable qualities only begin to explain Caldecott's supremacy. For me, his greatness lies in the wholeness of his personal vision of life. There is no emasculation of truth in his world. It is a green, vigorous world rendered faithfully and honestly in shades of dark and light, a world where the tragic and the joyful coexist, the one coloring the other. It encompasses three slaphappy huntsmen, as well as the ironic death of a mad, misunderstood dog; it allows for country lads and lasses flirting and dancing around the Maypole, as well as Baby Bunting's startled realization that his rabbit skin came from a creature that was once alive.

Caldecott never tells half-truths about life, and his honest vision, expressed with such conviction and robust energy, is one that children instinctively recognize and appreciate as true to their own lives.

Maurice Sendak
Ridgefield, Connecticut

A QUEST FOR CALDECOTT

BY ELIZABETH T. BILLINGTON

The wind was strong at my back, carrying with it spring rain. To escape its fury I ran as fast as I could through the darkness across the cobbled courtyard of the Victoria Hotel in Whitchurch, Shropshire. Breathless and blown, I burst through the side door into the public bar. Several men standing at the bar turned and stared. Thinking to myself, I must look like a Caldecott scarecrow, I hung my coat on a hook in the corner and smoothed my hair.

I sat down in the spot I had discovered on my first visit to the pub. It was a dim corner where a familiar photograph of Randolph Caldecott stared unobserved across the room. In this out-of-the-way spot I could sit and watch the local people as they gathered to discuss the events of the day.

I made my way to the bar and ordered some refreshment. Returning to the table I sat down, turned to the photograph and as I lifted my glass, said softly, "To us!"

Suddenly, I heard a man's voice say, "Is that who you've come to this part of the world to see?"

Startled, I turned. A young man, hands in his pockets, stood grinning at me. Squinting, he leaned toward the picture.

"Can't say I know him m'self," he said, and added cordially, "May I join you?"

I agreed that he could and we introduced ourselves.

"Now introduce your friend," he said, indicated the photograph.

"That is Randolph Caldecott. He was a very famous illustrator of children's books."

"And what's he doing here? Seems an odd place for a fellow like him."

"Not really. He was a bank clerk in Whitchurch in the 1860s before going to London to work as an artist. Between 1878 and 1885 he illustrated sixteen books with a style that was so new and different that his work really changed the whole course of children's picture books. Actually, he broke all the old rules of drawing for children and established new ones . . ."

"Oh, ho, I can see you like this man!" said my new companion. He stood up, rested his hand on the wall and took a closer look at the photograph.

"He looks such a serious and gentle person in the photograph, doesn't he?" I said. "But, don't let that fool you. He had great humor, joy, and compassion stored in that head. Come, look at the sketches on the other walls of this pub and you will see some of the fun shown in his work."

We walked slowly around the pub examining the illustrations from *Diana Wood's Wedding* and *How Tankerville Smith Got a Country Place*, drawn by Caldecott for a popular magazine of the late 1800s.

15

Returning from Church, Diana Wood's wedding

When we were seated again, I explained that it seemed quite appropriate for me to find Caldecott drawings decorating the walls of a pub. After all, Caldecott had loved to sketch people having fun. These feelings of gaiety and enjoyment thread their way through all of Caldecott's work. I explained that although I must have *known* that all along, it was only when I had come here that I *realized* it.

I told my friend how I had been raised on Caldecott books. As a child I had accepted his pictures as part of my growing up just as I accepted my neighborhood,

my school, my town. They were part of my childhood, part of me. Because the pictures could be seen again and again by simply opening one of his books, I was always able to renew my delight in their charm and freshness.

Some time ago I learned that the *Picture Books* were slowly going out of print. Thinking what a loss it would be if future generations could not enjoy Caldecott's wonderful talent, I decided to undertake a quest to find out more about the man himself. There was little biographical material available about Caldecott,

16

How Tankerville Smith took a Country Cottage

Alone at Club towards end of August Young T. S. reads beautiful description of "Gentleman's small Bijou Country Residence" to let, &c. IDEA! nothing to do, don't want a house; but go down & see it.

Approaches the place

so I had come to England to seek out information for myself.

Although the city of Chester in Cheshire, where Caldecott was born on March 22, 1846, was not unfamiliar to me, I had returned there with a new purpose in mind. I wished to step back in time and recapture the feeling of life in that city when Caldecott was young.

Caldecott was born on Bridge Street, which even today has unique Rows which are raised covered walks along the first-floor level joining the buildings. Many stairways lead from the Rows to the street below.

With a little imagination, I could picture boys and girls of long ago enjoying games of hide-and-go-seek in the Rows.

I pored over stacks of the town records and discovered that Caldecott's father, John Caldecott, was a woolen draper, tailor, and hatter who carried on his business in the Rows. Like many other families in the business of selling cloth, their living quarters were on the floors above the shop.

From a description given by his younger brother, Alfred, I was able to conceive a mental picture of the artist as a boy. Due to an early siege of rheumatic

17

fever, Randolph was characterized as "always delicate." However, his talent was quick to come to the surface, and even at the age of six he could be found sketching scenes or figures.

Caldecott attended the King's School, which was the Grammar School then attached to the Chester Cathedral. Since 1541 the school had been housed in the Refectory adjacent to the cathedral. History tells us that the school did not number twenty pupils in all. I wondered if the headmaster, Mr. James Harris, had enjoyed having the slight boy with the brown curly hair and gentle gray-blue eyes in the school. What did Harris think of this youngster who liked to draw, make models in clay, and whittle away in wood? Had Headmaster Harris been the person who arranged for Caldecott to attend the now nonexistent Chester School of Art for instruction in drawing? So far I have not found the answer to these questions, but I did find delight in an original watercolor drawing of the Refectory when it was used as a school. This drawing that Caldecott made long ago with love and care may still be found on the wall in the back of the Refectory.

The cathedral has been remodeled since Caldecott's time, but in the north transept there is a memorial tablet to Caldecott. I stood in the quiet cathedral, looking toward the altar, and easily imagined the pupils of the King's School sitting in the hand-carved choir stalls. Caldecott probably spent his time carefully studying those carvings instead of listening to the sermon. Certainly he was recalling his choir days when he made the drawing for the cathedral on Christmas Eve in *Old Christmas*.

My wanderings took me outside the walled city of Chester, but I found new homes instead of the farms and lanes Caldecott would have seen when he was a boy. Most of the old buildings in Hoole, a town that borders the Chester wall, have been taken down. Much to my disappointment, I was unable to find the house in Hamilton Street where Caldecott's mother, Mary

Dinah Brookes Caldecott, died of fever in August 1852.

However, I was able to locate the Queen Hotel on City Road just opposite the railroad station. This hotel had suffered a disastrous fire in November 1861, and Caldecott had recorded the event in a drawing. This drawing was published in the *Illustrated London News* on December 7, 1861; and it marked the first time Caldecott had seen his work in print. The unsigned drawing clearly shows the artist's ability to capture the excitement of the fire. No doubt the picture's publication motivated Caldecott to continue sketching enthusiastically in his spare time.

As I continued my travels, I again journeyed just outside Chester to Eaton Hall, where today stands a stately pair of wrought-iron gates. These gates date back to the early eighteenth century, and they so impressed Caldecott that he carefully reproduced them in an illustration for *Old Christmas*.

"I came to Whitchurch," I told my companion, "because Caldecott came here in 1861." I went on to explain that Caldecott had taken a job as a clerk with the Whitchurch and Ellesmere Bank. We talked awhile longer, mostly about Whitchurch and the surrounding countryside. Then the hour grew late and it was time to go our separate ways—my friend to his home in Wales, and I to continue my quest for Caldecott in Whitchurch.

In the days that followed, I was filled with delight each time I walked up the busy High Street and saw the graceful tower of the old Parish Church topping the hill. Even after all this time, there had been few changes in the church building. The porch had been added the year after Caldecott departed from Whitchurch and does not appear in his drawings. It is probable that he preferred to remember the church building as he knew it when he lived in Whitchurch.

I wondered what else would remain in the old market town a century after Caldecott's time. There were still

Destruction by fire of the Queen Railway Hotel in the Illustrated London News, *December 7, 1861,*
Caldecott's first published drawing

*Tower of Whitchurch Parish Church,
Whitchurch, Salop*

Porch and gates of Whitchurch Parish Church

*Antiquated buildings and signs in market
area of Whitchurch*

Hotel showing balcony and milestone, Whitchurch

Tower of Whitchurch Parish Church, as shown in The Great Panjandrum Himself

antiquated buildings in the market area, and old-fashioned picture signs extending into the narrow streets. At the door of the hotel stands an old mile-stone noting the distance from Chester. The entrance of the hotel is covered by an old-fashioned balcony of the kind Caldecott liked to draw. In the center of all this, a modern building on High Street stands out. In it I discovered the Caldecott Library and was able to read letters written by Caldecott when he lived in Whitchurch and Manchester. They revealed a happy young man enjoying himself with his friends, planning parties, sharing private jokes.

I knew that Caldecott had lived about two miles outside of the town on a farm at Wirswall and wasted no time taking a trip there. I walked the lanes as he had when he went to and from his work at the bank, and observed that the tower of the Parish Church appears at various angles as the hill rises and the road turns. Now I could understand how these images were imprinted on Caldecott's mind. From a stile, the same design as the one used by the Tattered Man, I watched blackbirds gather and rise in a patterned flight. I enjoyed thinking that it must have been their ancestors Caldecott had watched, remembered, and used in his *Picture Books*. Returning to town, I rested awhile on the wall of the churchyard. Down High Street, the recently remodeled building that had housed the bank in which Caldecott worked was clearly visible.

Friendships formed by Caldecott when he lived here came to my mind. Some of those friends had kept in touch with him for the rest of his life. It was from letters that Caldecott had written to these friends that I was able to form a sharper picture of him. One friend, James M. Etches, told this story of Caldecott's days in Whitchurch:

While working at the bank in Whitchurch, Caldecott, like other bank clerks of that time, accepted an agency for a life insurance company. Caldecott had no luck in making a sale. However, after a number of tries, he finally interested a rather wary farmer in insuring his life for 500 pounds. The forms were carefully filled out and sent on to the insurance company for their approval.

When the policy had been approved by the insurance company, they forwarded it to Caldecott. The farmer was told that the arrangements had been completed and was asked to bring the first payment. When he did so, he put the money on the counter and it was a beaming Caldecott who told the farmer the policy was his. Just as Caldecott was about to pick up the money the farmer lowered his huge hand over it.

"Now look'ere, Mr. Caldecott, let us understand each other; let there be no mistake," he said. "As I understand it, if I pay this money, and am alive and well this day twelvemonth, your company will pay me 500 pounds."

"Oh, dear, no!" replied Caldecott. "If you die before that time your representatives will receive the 500 pounds."

"Ah, well," said the farmer, pocketing the money, "that is not good enough for me! I shan't have anything to do with it." Out he stalked, leaving an open-mouthed young Caldecott standing at the counter.

It was the practice of the bank to carry on much of its trading in the farmhouses and old halls near Whitchurch. By going out to these farms and halls, Caldecott grew to know and love the countryside and towns nearby. He had a pleasant disposition and soon was made welcome whether he was on a business call or just stopping by for a casual chat. The friends he made while conducting business for the bank soon invited him to join the hunt, ride the steeplechase, and attend country dances.

I roamed country lanes, explored hidden hamlets and old halls, trying to see them through Caldecott's eyes. One morning before the mist had burned off, I started in search of yet another landmark made familiar to me by Caldecott. It was the buttressed tower

To the Angel

Old houses and tower of Whitchurch used in Elegy on the Death of a Mad Dog

of the church in Malpas, Cheshire, not far from Whit-church.

To my surprise I had to ease the car into a procession of horses, horse vans, and cars moving along the narrow road. By chance I had timed my visit to Malpas the same day that a steeplechase was to be held outside the town. Farmers in their heavy boots had stopped their work to stand by the roadside and watch. Windows of the scattered houses were open wide and women leaned out waving and watching. Sitting on farm gates, wide-eyed children stared at the procession and called out greetings as friends passed. The noise of a hunter's horn carried across the open country,

adding to the excitement. As I moved on, I suddenly saw Caldecott's tower come into view as it stood on a gentle hill. The town settled snug and close about it, and the vigilant brass cock atop the buttressed tower seemed to call a welcome across the fields.

A holiday mood had seized the old town. Round-faced rosy children pranced along the stones to join the merriment. A modern "fair lady" sat astride her horse passing buildings that remained from Caldecott's time. I managed to leave the steeplechase crowds and climbed the hill to the old church. At the entrance to the graveyard of St. Oswald's Church, I found the iron gates and rounded steps recorded by Calde-

Old houses and tower of Whitchurch Parish Church

Present-day stile near Whitchurch

Stile pictured in
The House that Jack Built

Tower of St. Oswald's Parish Church, and town of Malpas, Cheshire

*Tower of St. Oswald's Parish Church, and
town of Malpas as pictured by Caldecott in* Baby Bunting

Tower of St. Oswald's Parish Church, and town of Malpas in The Fox Jumps over the Parson's Gate

Tower of St. Oswald's Parish Church as pictured in Jackanapes

Tower of St. Oswald's Parish Church on a Christmas greeting

46 Gt. Russell St. Bloomsbury.

*Tower of St. Oswald's Parish Church, and gates shown in different position
in* Ride a Cock Horse to Banbury Cross

cott in many and various ways. The gates are works of art that date back to the early seventeenth century and have fortunately survived the wars. The church building is itself a gem that has been lovingly cared for over the years. A few box pews remain, and the sight of Mrs. Mary Blaize slumbering in the corner of one would have been no surprise.

In the graveyard, cut into stones smoothed by time, I found memorials to Caldecotts of an earlier era. Indeed, the Caldecott name is an old one in this area and I could understand why Caldecott had been sent to this part of the country to work. No doubt his father, concerned about young Randolph's health, had sent him back to where the family had been known to benefit from the fresh air and good food of the rich farming country. The rheumatic fever that had weakened his heart as a child recurred from time to time for the rest of his life. He often made references to his health when writing friends, but he did not complain, just accepted his illness as a way of life.

Had my visit to Whitchurch and Malpas brought me any closer to Caldecott? It had, I felt. Seeing places he had loved, meeting people not very different from those he had known, I could understand his attachment to this place.

In 1867, when he was twenty-one, Caldecott left Whitchurch to join the Manchester and Salford Bank in Manchester. As the move to Whitchurch had enlarged Caldecott's horizon, so the move to Manchester opened yet another new world to him. How exciting

27

Buttressed steeple, St. Oswald's, Malpas

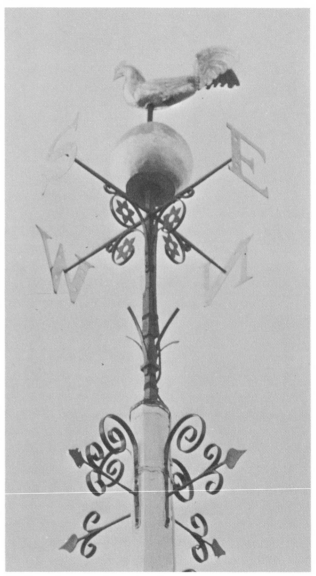

Churchyard memorial, St. Oswald's, Malpas

Vigilant brass cock on weather vane,
St. Oswald's, Malpas (photograph by C. Barlow)

28

A modern fair lady riding to the steeplechase in Malpas, Cheshire

Steps and gates of St. Oswald's Parish Church, Malpas, Cheshire

29

Mrs. Mary Blaize slumbering in her pew from An Elegy on the Glory of her Sex, Mrs. Mary Blaize

Children parade past the gates from The Great Panjandrum Himself

and stimulating it must have been for him to finally meet people who appreciated his ability to sketch, people who encouraged him to develop his broad artistic talents by attending school at night. Soon, he seemed to be swept along in a tide of sketching, painting, and modeling in clay, while his work at the bank became quite secondary.

Encouraged because his drawings were being published in local weeklies and exhibited in galleries, he decided in the spring of 1870 to take some sketches to London. Although his visit was short, he left a few of the drawings from his portfolio with Thomas Armstrong. Armstrong was a well-known artist of the time. He had been born in Fallowfield, Manchester, where he had first studied before going to the Continent to work further. Although Armstrong was fourteen years Caldecott's senior, the two men became intimate friends and remained so until Caldecott's death sixteen years later.

Returning to Manchester, Caldecott continued to work at the bank and practice sketching at night. But all the time London beckoned with its enticing opportunities to study, learn, and work. In 1872, after selling several drawings to Henry Blackburn, editor of the magazine *London Society,* he yielded to the enticement. Manchester and the bank were left behind. Caldecott devoted the remaining fourteen years of his life to art.

I, too, heeded the call of London and followed Caldecott to the busy, noisy, gray city. I had read of all the work accomplished by Caldecott in those first years and wondered how I could possibly sort it out.

Through Armstrong, Caldecott met Sir Edward J. Poynter, a painter and member of the Royal Academy. In 1871 Poynter had been chosen professor of the newly established Slade Chair and School at University College, London. With great enthusiasm Caldecott joined a life class under his instruction.

Armstrong also introduced Caldecott to other well-known artists, James Whistler, Thomas Lamont, and Sir John Gilbert. He met George du Maurier, who was a writer as well as an artist in black-and-white drawings, and Comyns-Carr, the editor, critic and playwright. All were part of the surging creative force in London. They liked young Caldecott and welcomed him into their midst.

Reading about these people and their time, I began to feel that London was much like a small town. Everyone seemed to know everyone else. They visited socially, discussed their work, and helped one another. Mail service was rapid; letters went back and forth with ease. From the correspondence that has been preserved, I gathered information and a feeling for the time.

Caldecott eagerly took advantage of every opportunity to develop his talent. With his friend Thomas Armstrong, he accepted a commission to paint decorative panels for Bank House, the home of Henry Renshaw at Chapel-en-le-Frith, where they may be found today. The panels were executed in oil on canvas during 1872 and 1873. For his part of the work, Caldecott was to paint a series of elaborate birds for which he had to make a careful study of anatomical details and colors. This commission served to introduce Caldecott to a wealthy patron and allowed Armstrong to teach Caldecott as they worked together. Another opportunity arose when he met Jules Dalou, the French sculptor. Dalou was having trouble teaching because of his poor English. Caldecott worked out an agreement: in return for his help in improving M. Dalou's English, Caldecott would receive instruction in clay modeling.

In a diary he kept, Caldecott noted that he had made "a cat crouching for a spring" while working with M. Dalou. Surely this experience influenced him when later he made the unforgettable drawing of the

A fine lady on a white horse as portrayed by Caldecott in Ride a Cock Horse to Banbury Cross

crouched cat in *The House that Jack Built.* Thinking about his modeling, painting in oils, and creating bas reliefs, I began to wonder if Caldecott could ever have been idle for a minute.

It was Henry Blackburn, the editor of *London Society,* who first encouraged Caldecott to channel his abilities into becoming an illustrator. Caldecott was adept at catching a situation quickly and putting it on paper, a most important trait in an illustrator of current news stories in the days before the camera was used for newspaper pictures. However, Blackburn was aware of Caldecott's poor health, and he felt Caldecott should avoid the pressures of journalistic work. He suggested instead that Caldecott illustrate books of

travel, which would make it possible for Caldecott to spend the winters in warmer climates than England.

In association with Blackburn, Caldecott illustrated several books. The first was *The Harz Mountains: A Tour in the Toy Country.* This book introduced Caldecott's work to the American public when it appeared in *Harper's New Monthly Magazine* in New York in June of 1873. Through the efforts of Blackburn, Caldecott's sketches of the Vienna International Exhibition appeared in the September 16, 1873 *New York Daily Graphic.*

I was interested to learn that Blackburn, who was an author, critic, and lecturer, was considered to be the terror of artists. He originated the idea of illus-

A debating society

trated catalogs for art exhibitions and would demand black-and-white sketches of an artist's work for inclusion in the catalogs. Despite his reputation as a difficult person to get along with, he and Caldecott were not only collaborators but also friends.

Certainly, as a close friend, Blackburn was aware of Caldecott's dislike of publicity and his wish for privacy in his personal life. Even so, Blackburn wrote a memoir entitled *Randolph Caldecott: A Personal Memoir of His Early Art Career,* published in London in 1886. Today we can be grateful that he went against Caldecott's wishes, for it is only through Blackburn's work that we have a record of Caldecott's early development as an artist.

"A Debating Society" was one of the first of Caldecott's drawings to be used by Blackburn and appeared in *London Society* in 1871. It was engraved for publication by James D. Cooper. In January of 1874 Cooper called on Caldecott in his studio. The engraver brought with him a copy of Washington Irving's *Old Christmas.*

Cooper was a breezy and jovial man in his early fifties who called himself "the old woodpecker." Caldecott, on the other hand, was in his middle twen-

ties, just beginning to feel success as an artist. With a bit of imagination, one can picture them on a cold, dark January day going over the book. Cooper had been trying for a long time to find an artist to illustrate Irving's work. In an effort to interest Caldecott, Cooper did not underestimate the size of the task if Caldecott were to agree to make the drawings and Cooper to do the wood engraving.

Cooper left the book with Caldecott so he might consider it at his leisure. Perhaps it was too cold and wet for Caldecott to venture out of doors that day, so he picked up the book and read it once more. As he did, his enthusiasm grew. He started to work almost immediately and concentrated on the illustrations for most of 1874. As he concentrated on this project, he began to see results of his years of diligent study.

Caldecott, who had been born with a unique appreciation of humor and the joy of living, also had great natural ability as a painter and sculptor. As he prepared the illustrations for Irving's work with his newly mastered skills, his humor and joy burst forth, were nurtured and released into his work. From Caldecott's memory came scenes of his life in Shropshire. The people, places, animals, and houses he loved

Caldecott depicts himself growing weary of listening to James D. Cooper reading complimentary reviews of Old Christmas

blended with Irving's feel for England, formed during a visit many years earlier.

Cooper spent almost a year engraving Caldecott's work. In November 1875, *Old Christmas: Selections from The Sketch Book* was published by Macmillan and Company. Almost immediately Caldecott's work was acclaimed everywhere. He was hailed as a talented illustrator and artist. With his characteristic spirit of fun, Caldecott pretended to grow tired of the repeated praise and sketched himself listening to Cooper as he read the complimentary reviews.

Because he felt so much at home with Irving's work, Caldecott went on to illustrate *Bracebridge Hall: Selections from The Sketch Book,* which was published by Macmillan in 1876. This, too, was well received by both reviewers and the public.

The first part of my time in London was devoted to the British Museum. I spent a day in the Print Room examining original artwork of Caldecott, and many days in the Library enjoying old issues of *Graphic, London Society,* and other periodicals in which Caldecott's work appeared. One afternoon, as I waited for another magazine to come from the shelves, I was troubled by a feeling that, despite all the reading and examining of sketches, I still did not feel any closer to the real Caldecott.

That evening as I left, I stopped outside 46 Great Russell Street, just opposite the museum. Caldecott had lived and worked in this building for the first six years of his art career. On impulse I entered the premises, the lower floors of which were now occupied by a business firm.

The present occupant, a young woman, greeted me and rather awkwardly I explained the reason for my interest in the building. As I spoke, my explanation sounded strange even to me, and I wondered if this stranger would understand my feelings. Fortunately,

Where Caldecott lived and worked from 1872 until 1879, 46 Great Russell Street, London

my fears were quickly allayed and I was warmly welcomed into the house. The woman explained that she lived on the upper floors and also shared my fascination with the building. She knew a great deal about the history of the place, and I was delighted by the tour around the house that she gave me. I was shown the original wooden staircase and railings that still remain in place and I climbed the narrow, turning stairs to the upper rooms where Caldecott must have had his studio. Yes, in this atmosphere I felt I could share the artist's thoughts.

I left the building in the dusk, feeling closer to Caldecott than I had since leaving Whitchurch. As I walked back to my hotel, I decided that the best way for me to trace Caldecott in London was through the way I had first known him—children's books.

One cannot think of children's books in the mid and late 1800s without thinking of Edmund Evans. A most talented wood engraver and color printer, Evans had a tremendous imagination as well as an astute sense of business. It has always seemed a shame to me that Evans never kept a diary as a young man. His *Reminiscences* give one the feeling that he may have forgotten a good deal about his early days as a wood engraver and printer. I believe that had he kept a diary when he was twenty-one and just completing his seven-year apprenticeship to Ebenezer Landells, we would have a different picture of both the man and of the times.

From descriptions I have read, I can see him a tall and thin young man, perky and full of ideas. No doubt his first adventure in printing picture books for children was purely commercial in intention. The early books were printed in black and white, and dabs of color were added by hand by poorly paid youngsters. When Evans saw the success of these books, his business intuition led him to seize on it. He quickly realized that children's books would be an ever-expanding field for his talents as a wood engraver and printer.

Another change was also happening at this time. Bookstalls were beginning to appear in railway stations. With his keen commercial sense, Evans saw these as likely places for extending the market for children's books. He started to print these books in blue and red ink on white paper, but it did not take Evans long to observe that the white cover was too quickly soiled. Just as today, no one wanted to buy a book with a smudged cover. Hence, he quickly substituted a yellow paper with a shiny, coated surface. The books were immediately successful and were affectionately called "yellow backs," or more humorously, "mustard plasters." By Caldecott's time Evans was a well-established color printer, reproducing delicate colors from boxwood blocks.

Many of the surging social and economic changes that were taking place then in Britain grew out of the fact that more and more people were becoming literate. As the number of people who could read grew, the interest in books spread. Changes in the publishing industry developed as part of the transition. Catchpenny publishers were slowly being replaced by people of more education. Individuals with more modern attitudes and ideas entered the book field. Quite naturally, these changes also affected children's books. Slowly but surely good writers and gifted artists turned their talents to books for young readers.

Edmund Evans, like other wood engravers and printers, initiated much of the work that kept his presses busy. Evans would approach an artist with an idea for a book. If the artist was agreeable, they would develop the idea and the artist would go ahead with the drawings. Evans in turn would take the book to a publisher, and when successful in selling it he would go ahead with the printing. The finished sheets would be delivered to the publisher by Evans.

From Evans' writings I knew that he also had visited Caldecott's studio in Great Russell Street. It was not difficult to imagine their meeting. Edmund Evans, twenty years older than Caldecott, was looking for a new artist to illustrate for children. He had seen the illustrations for *Old Christmas* and had been fascinated by them. Hence, when Evans met with Caldecott, he reasoned that the artist's rich store of happy memories of life in a small country town could be used in illustrating old rhymes for children. Evans recalled that it was not until some time later, when Caldecott

Edmund Evans (on right) as the "ruffian strong" in The Babes in the Wood

was visiting the Evans home at Witley, that they finally agreed to combine their skills to produce *John Gilpin* and *The House that Jack Built.*

Again, the relationship was not merely a business one, and the two men became fast friends. Evans understood, appreciated, and encouraged the young artist to express himself fully in his illustrations. Undoubtedly Evans' sympathy for Caldecott added to the quality of the final artwork, for the wood engraver stands between the artist and the printed picture. If the artist is to come through with clarity, the engraver

must value the artist's ability and bring his own insight to bear on what the artist has created.

It is interesting to speculate that had Caldecott not listened to Evans and not been persuaded to illustrate children's rhymes, he might today be known only as a fine but minor artist. In fact, many of the turning points in Caldecott's life were a result of the people who befriended him after being impressed by his work.

In his reminiscences about the *Picture Books*, Evans recalled the tremendous sale they had enjoyed. For my part, I wondered what kind of critical reception

Caldecott portrayed himself as the "gentleman of good account" in The Babes in the Wood

they had received. In the newspaper files of The New York Public Library I found the answer. *The Nation* for December 19, 1878, published in New York, reviewed new books for children, probably in time for Christmas buying. The reviewer observed:

Mr. R. Caldecott's latest caricatures should not be overlooked by purveyors for the nursery. His "John Gilpin" and "The House that Jack Built" (Routledge) are sui generis, *and irresistibly funny as well as clever. One hardly knows which to admire most—the full page color-prints, or the outline sketches in the brown ink of the text. Happy the generation that is brought up on such masters as Mr. Caldecott and Mr. Walter Crane.*

Probably it was also Evans who put forward the idea that Caldecott next illustrate the old rhyme, *The*

Babes in the Wood, which had been issued as one of *Aunt Mavor's Everlasting Toy Books* (Routledge, Warne and Routledge) in 1860. Edmund Evans had engraved the illustrations for that edition, and they had been colored by hand. Perhaps Evans was curious to see what Caldecott would do with the old rhyme.

Caldecott had some fun with Evans, using him as the model for one of the "ruffians strong." As the "gentlemen of good account, sore sick and like to die," Caldecott cast himself. Unfortunately, the reviewer for *The Nation* (December 18, 1879) was not at all pleased with the illustrations. "The artist has shown a grievous want of taste in treating humorously the tragedy of the Babes," he complained. Perhaps he did not know that Caldecott himself was "sore sick and like to die" but still was able to treat the matter unoppressively. No matter, Caldecott did not let himself be deterred by the reviewer's comments.

38

In 1877 his close friend Thomas Armstrong took Caldecott to the home of another young artist, Walter Crane. Crane was already successful and had been illustrating books for a dozen years. He was famous in Europe as well as in England for the drawings he made for children. As it happened, both he and Caldecott were about the same age and had much in common. They both came from old Chester families, although Crane had not been brought up in the old city. Crane was familiar with Whitchurch, for two of his aunts had run a school there. In contrast to Caldecott, Crane came from a family of artists who had fostered his talent and developed it with practical direction. The two young men found much to talk about in their past experiences and present-day interests, and Caldecott's friendship with Crane was to be a lifelong one.

In his book, *An Artist's Reminiscences,* Crane has some fond recollections of his friend. In particular, Crane notes that Caldecott would ride over on horseback in the early evening so that he could play with Crane's children before their bedtime.

Crane's book helped me to round out my picture of Caldecott's personality. He described Caldecott as tall and handsome, with light brown hair and gray-blue eyes. It was from Crane I learned that Caldecott's voice was low and gentle, that his manner was quiet and rather serious. Crane felt that Caldecott's earnest manner of speaking hid the extraordinary vivacity and humor revealed in his drawings, and that Caldecott's occasional funny remarks showed only the surface of a much deeper sense of humor.

Soon after Caldecott met Crane, he started work on *John Gilpin* and *The House that Jack Built.* Together they had discussed the way in which Caldecott could arrange to collect a royalty on the *Picture Books.* Crane had never received a royalty for his many toy books. This was because custom did not call for one to be paid and Crane was not one to try to change the

royalty practices. However, the fact that Caldecott expected royalties indicated that attitudes were changing in the publishing field.

Not only did he expect royalties, Caldecott later became dissatisfied with the amount he was being paid and complained to Edmund Evans. The prices of books had only just started their upward trend, and Evans felt that sales would suffer if the prices increased even more. Hence, he persuaded Caldecott of the wisdom of keeping the price of the books and the royalties low.

What else did Caldecott and Crane talk about on those evening visits? Did they discuss the signing of their work? Crane used a rebus to sign his pictures, Caldecott a plain R C, fitted into the sketch. Caldecott once wrote in a letter: ". . . as for myself I would rather leave out my initials than to have them interfere with the drawing—and I often do—and in these slight drawings every little tells."

We shall never know if the two artists talked about illustrating for children although it seems likely that they did. We only know that when Caldecott began working on his illustrations for *John Gilpin* and *The House that Jack Built,* he broke the bounds set by his predecessors. He did not decorate the stories, he interpreted them. The heavy black borders that once confined the illustrations were gone. Caldecott's figures leap, dance, run, and chase from page to page. Their joy is unrestricted! His gift of humor is ageless. School children of today have told me, "What I like best is when John Gilpin goes so fast he breaks the bottles!" or "I like the milkmaid best. She's pretty, and I didn't expect her to be so funny!"

At the same time that Caldecott entered the field of children's books, Kate Greenaway started illustrating for the same audience. In her, Caldecott found another friend, and they visited each other as well as exchanged letters. Both illustrators used the same models and they discussed the technical problems that

*Caldecott's sketch of children
in Kate Greenaway's style*

grew out of Caldecott's use of a brown ink that was not waterproof. Kate Greenaway's letters reveal her envy of Caldecott's imagination, which allowed him to enlarge and develop a verse through pictures. On one occasion when they were both guests in the home of a mutual friend, Caldecott made—as a joke—a sketch to show that overnight he had lost his own style and that all his sketches were coming out like Kate Greenaway's. Fortunately, Greenaway did not take offense at this action; rather, she cherished the little sketch for the rest of her life.

In June of 1879, Caldecott met Mrs. Juliana Horatia Ewing, who was one of the most respected authors of children's books of the time. Mrs. Ewing was only five years older than Caldecott and she, too, suffered from ill health. However, the two greatest similarities between Caldecott and Mrs. Ewing were their mutual ability to see every character as a real live person and their strong sense of the dramatic. Caldecott expressed drama in line and design, Mrs. Ewing in the construction of her stories.

On meeting Caldecott, Mrs. Ewing immediately

asked him to do the graphics for one of her stories. *Jackanapes* was only an idea in her mind at that time, but she suggested to him how he might illustrate the story. Some years passed before the work could be fitted into his crowded schedule. Because of the delay, Caldecott and Mrs. Ewing exchanged letters during this period of time. Caldecott's replies reveal the growing pressure of his work, as well as an artist giving careful attention to each small detail. Ultimately, Caldecott illustrated several other stories for Mrs. Ewing.

I was especially interested in one letter in which Mrs. Ewing discussed the illustrations for *Sing A Song for Sixpence*. By coincidence I had learned that two of the original drawings for this rhyme had been purchased by Rupert Potter, the father of Beatrix Potter, the author-illustrator of *The Tale of Peter Rabbit*. At one time Mr. Potter had owned about thirty Caldecott originals, and therefore Beatrix could study Caldecott's drawings firsthand. She tried, in 1896, to copy some of his drawings but with little success. In her

Caldecott portrayed himself anticipating life in his country house, Wybournes (near Sevenoaks, Kent)

bedroom at Hilltop in Sawrey, England, still hang two watercolors from *Sing A Song for Sixpence,* a bridge between two artists who each found a secure place illustrating books for children in their own unique way.

Caldecott worked long and hard, perhaps too hard for his own well-being. In 1876 his first painting was hung at the Royal Academy, but in November of the same year his health was so poor the doctor had to send him away for a rest. The realization that he must slow his pace, as well as his love of country life, may be what prompted Caldecott to buy a country house. In 1879 he purchased Wybournes at Kemsing, a small village near Sevenoaks in Kent.

I wanted very much to see Kemsing. As luck would have it, I had met another admirer of Caldecott, Michael Hutchins. As of this writing, Mr. Hutchins teaches the history of printing at Camberwell College and lives in Kent, near Kemsing. Hence, one fine autumn afternoon in 1972 we went "Caldecotting" together.

Our first stop was the Church of St. Martin-of-Tours in Chelsfield, Kent, another church and tower not unfamiliar to me. I had seen it first on a letter Caldecott had sent to a friend telling of the plans for his marriage to Marian H. Brind on March 18, 1880.

Mr. Hutchins has established that the Brind family lived in the house adjacent to the church and that Marian Brind had walked to her wedding. Caldecott's brother, the Reverend Alfred Caldecott, assisted in the ceremony. In the walking weddings pictured in *The Great Panjandrum Himself* and *The Fox Jumps over the Parson's Gate,* it is quite possible that Caldecott drew on the memory of his own happy wedding. There is certainly a resemblance between the stone porch in his drawing and that of St. Martin-of-Tours.

Caldecott's home, Wybournes, in Kemsing (near Sevenoaks, Kent)

The Church of St. Martin-of-Tours, Chels-field, Kent. Here Caldecott and Marian Harriet Brind were married

My dear Clough,

"There were 3 ravens sat on a tree;" but the above 3 are not ravens. Somebody's going to stop — or put a stopper—on 1 of the 3. It is the 1 in the middle. He only seems quite alive to the seriousness & severity & gravity of the occasion. The 3 are waiting until what they consider are the proper moment for entering the adjacent church & taking up their stands at the Hymeneal altar — and its the middle 1 who's to be wed. This waiting on a rail has not taken place yet. It is a

Wybournes, Kemsing, nr Sevenoaks 11 March 1880 10.30PM

Stone porch and entrance used by Caldecott in The Fox Jumps over the Parson's Gate

Above: through this gate Marian Brind walked to her wedding

Left: stone porch and entrance of Church of St. Martin-of-Tours

A walking wedding from The Great Panjandrum Himself

Having spent a pleasant hour exploring the church, we drove on through the lanes Caldecott had traveled, either in a dogcart or on horseback, when courting Marian Brind. Along the Pilgrim's Way we rode, down Childsbridge Road into the small village of Kemsing, which seemed untouched by the busy world outside. Mr. Hutchins had established the location of the house called Wybournes, which had been destroyed about the turn of the century. We walked beside the old brick wall, which is all that remains today. Standing on tiptoe, it was possible for us to peek over the wall and see where the house had been and trace the remains of the gardens.

I have long enjoyed the humor and variety of *A Sketch Book of R. Caldecott's*, published in 1883 by George Routledge. But only as I relaxed in the warm autumn sun on a low part of that crumbling wall did I realize how intimate a pictorial diary the *Sketch Book* was of the Caldecotts' life there.

I let my mind wander and imagined the young lady shown ready to serve tea in the garden could be Marian Caldecott. Did Caldecott look up from his work one morning to see Marian talking with the old gardener and feel it was a scene he wished to preserve on paper? I had no doubt that he was recalling a game of lawn tennis with friends in another sketch. I rose lazily from the wall and strolled over the down where he and Marian must have ridden on horseback. One winter sport they most certainly enjoyed together was ice skating with neighbors and friends. Caldecott's

45

Believed to be Marian Caldecott

Exercising the Pack

letters and his sketches of dogs—in repose or at play—also reflect the happiness found at Wybournes.

Caldecott wrote to friends that once he was married he kept regular hours. "Breakfast at eight—and no nonsense. Work from nine to two." The dogcart and gig he loved gave way to a more dignified horse and buggy. Caldecott was maturing as a man as well as an artist.

It was with regret that I left the site of Wybournes that fading autumn afternoon. The Caldecotts had left in 1882 and moved to London. In order for Randolph to have a permanent place in which to work, they had taken a long lease on a house near the South Kensington Museum (now the Victoria and Albert Museum). They planned to have another country home, however, and after much searching they found a house in Farnham, Surrey, where they thought the climate might be drier. Unfortunately neither the house nor the climate was satisfactory and both husband and wife were sorry they had left Wybournes.

On my return to London I set off to find 24 Holland Street in Kensington, where the Caldecotts had lived for five years. I discovered a small Georgian house with a crown-glass door. However, the present occupants were not at home, so I was not able to see the inside of the house. Hence, I decided to further my quest for Caldecott at the Victoria and Albert Museum.

I was pleased to examine the artist's proof for the original wood engravings for many of the *Picture Books*. Caldecott's notes to the printer reveal the close attention he paid to each detail.

At the museum I was also able to look through an engaging collection of sketches, some on scraps of waste paper, with letters collected by Caldecott's longtime friend William Clough. From these I learned

Repose

Play

that Caldecott had problems in proportion when first he sketched the human figure.

I had mixed emotions as I thumbed through Caldecott's small sketchbooks. The first sketchbook, started in 1872 when he first came to London at twenty-six, is inscribed inside the front cover in a boyish manner:

R. Caldecott, his book
46 Gt. Russell St. W C

The covers bear miscellaneous notes and addresses. Among the sketches of hands and feet, there is one of Caldecott himself with a young lady as they walk toward the familiar tower of the Parish Church at Whitchurch. Was the artist lonesome that first busy year in London, and did his thoughts sometimes return to Whitchurch and the happy times he had known there?

Examining the cataloging of the Caldecott materials, I realized that the small sketchbooks had come to the Victoria and Albert collection in 1932. This was the year of Marian Caldecott's death, forty-six years after her husband's. The books had been part of her private memorabilia until then.

49

*Caldecott pictures himself and
a young lady walking toward the
Parish Church in Whitchurch.*

Caldecott's London home, 24 Holland St., Kensington

Sketch from one of Caldecott's letters

*Drawings appear on many of Caldecott's letters.
Usually they encircled the address and seemed to
reveal his state of mind at the time far more clearly
than he may have known. These four (on opposite
page) appeared on letters to his friend Frederick
Locker-Lampson. The contentment of the time at
Wybournes is reflected in two of them*

In November of 1880 sixty thousand copies of his forth-coming Sing a Song for Sixpence *and* The Three Jovial Huntsmen *were to be printed. The sketch reveals that he anticipated the joy they would bring to readers*

The Broomfield sketch depicts Caldecott's unhappiness with that home. The Christmas of 1882 he and his wife spent with her family in Kent. In Broomfield Christmas went uncelebrated and a bird lies dead on the doorstep

The Christmas drawing of Caldecott and his wife sending off a Christmas messenger to Rowfant, the home of the Locker-Lampsons, discloses the happiness of the first Christmas after their marriage

The satisfaction of a good harvest of hay is shown in the sketch of Caldecott watching the haying at Broomfield on July 18, 1885

51

Our Haymaking

WE TAKE A COUNTRY COTTAGE
WITH THE ADJOINING MEADOW OF HAYGRASS

The last acquisition in the collection came from a member of the Brind family in 1951. It includes the originals of six sketches for *Our Haymaking*, which I had seen when looking at the Summer 1881 edition of the *Graphic*. Now I realized that these sketches portrayed the first haymaking of the newly wed Caldecotts at Wybournes. I grinned as I read Caldecott's pencil note in the margin of the picture "The Carrying." It read, "or the carrying on." I feel sure these originals and the small sketchbooks were cherished by Marian Caldecott, a happy time in their life.

The warmth I experienced in examining these pictures was washed away by a wave of sympathy for Marian Caldecott when I turned over the sketch "Negroes Loading Cotton Bales in Charleston." On the reverse I read, "Last drawing ever made by Ran-

52

THE CARRYING

dolph Caldecott." Marian Caldecott's loneliness and sorrow touched me. There had been no children, and her godson, the only son of Thomas Armstrong, died as a youth.

The next step in my quest had to be carried on in the United States, which proved no easy task. The Caldecotts had left the soggy, damp English winter each year. Usually they headed for the south of France or Italy. However, in October 1885, at the suggestion of their friends the Frederick Locker-Lampsons, Caldecott and his wife sailed for New York.

I have often puzzled over the reason for Caldecott's undertaking this trip. Locker-Lampson was a poet twenty-five years older than Caldecott. His second wife, Jane Locker, a writer, was a contemporary of the Caldecotts. Perhaps it was a desire for new horizons

53

Grave of Randolph Caldecott, Evergreen Cemetery, St. Augustine, Florida

that got them talking about America. I feel certain that neither of the Caldecotts truly understood how trying a rough ocean voyage could be, nor did they realize that they would be in a strange land with customs and climate far different than those they knew on the Continent or in England.

The planned sketching trip was to take them from New York to Philadelphia and down the East Coast. They were to spend the winter months in the warm southern part of the United States visiting Florida and New Orleans; later they would move on to California and Colorado. The long journey would end in Boston, Massachusetts. It was a strenuous and ambitious tour

for a man in frail health, but Randolph Caldecott started out in high spirits. Even the rough ocean crossing did not discourage him. He wrote friends with his usual good humor, saying he hoped an overland route would be discovered before they made their return voyage to England.

After a brief stay in New York, the Caldecotts visited Philadelphia. Then they moved on to Washington, D.C. and continued down the Coast, stopping at Charleston, where Randolph was still well enough to make a sketch.

By mid-December they were in St. Augustine, Florida. The unusually cold winter did not help the artist who was by now seriously ill. On January 14, 1886, Marian Caldecott wrote to Jane Locker-Lampson from the Magnolia Hotel in St. Augustine reporting that Randolph had been very ill through December, but was now improving and gaining strength. Marian felt that the weakness of his heart had complicated the illness, which she referred to as "a severe attack of gastritis."

In 1974 the St. Augustine Historical Society received a box of death certificates and burial records for the years 1878 through 1894. In that box was a plain piece of paper that reads:

This certifies that Mr. Randolph Caldecott age 39, Born in Chester Engd. died at St. Augustine, Fla. February 13, 1886, of organic disease of the heart.

> H. Caruthers
> Physician

Saturday
February 13, 1886

Thomas Armstrong wrote to Walter Crane on February 14 to report "the very bad news." Armstrong was shocked, for earlier reports had said that Caldecott

*Memorial tablet to
Randolph Caldecott designed
by Sir Alfred Gilbert, R.A.
in the artist's corner of
the crypt of St. Paul's
Cathedral, London, near
Cruikshank's tomb*

seemed to be recovering. Although Armstrong wished to go to Florida to help Marian Caldecott, it was not possible as the distance was too great. He asked her by cable whether she would like someone to come to St. Augustine. Her reply was, "No."

It was left to Marian Caldecott, alone in a foreign land, to arrange for her husband's burial. How strange it must have seemed to one used to English churchyards to have him buried in what was then a small cemetery in open country with but twenty other graves.

My quest took me to the Evergreen Cemetery, as it is now named, to find the grave. I walked slowly, under the tall palm trees, past blossoming azaleas, to a cedar tree where I found the tombstone. I stood in silence, deeply touched. I recalled a letter written by Marian Caldecott to Frederick Locker-Lampson in January of 1887. She discussed with him the plans for the memorial tablet in the crypt of St. Paul's Cathedral, London. The tablet, showing a demure Breton child holding Caldecott's picture, honors him still.

As does the world.

THE CALDECOTT MEDAL

The Caldecott Medal is awarded annually by the Association for Services to Children of the American Library Association. It is given to the illustrator of the most distinguished American picture book for children published in the United States during the preceding year.

From personal experience, I know that there was great excitement in both library and publishing fields when the medal was first established. In 1936 I had the uncertain distinction of becoming the newest, youngest, and only female employee of Frederick Warne in New York. The routine of the quiet Warne office was broken one afternoon with the hearty entrance of Frederick G. Melcher, then editor of *Publishers Weekly.* I listened carefully as he explained that he had come to order a complete set of *Caldecott Picture Books.* They were to be sent to the sculptor René Chambellan, who was to design the newly established Caldecott Medal, of which Mr. Melcher was the donor. As we walked into the Sample Room, Mr. Melcher picked up a *Caldecott Picture Book* from the display. He thumbed through it with delight and commented on the details that he admired in some of the sketches. Mr. Melcher told me he felt Caldecott held a unique place in the history of picture books, that he had ushered in a new age of illustration for children by giving them pictures filled with joy and beauty. One could not doubt that Mr. Melcher believed this spirit of joy was the goal illustrators of children's books should strive for in their work.

Mr. Chambellan spent a few days examining the books and was greatly impressed by Caldecott's skill as an artist. He decided that the finest tribute would be to use two pictures from Caldecott's work—one for each side of the medal.

While preparing this article about the Caldecott Medal, I examined a brochure published by the American Library Association. There I noted it was referred to as the Randolph *J.* Caldecott Medal and I was puzzled by this reference since I knew it was common for an English person not to have a middle name. Indeed, a copy of Caldecott's birth certificate gave his name simply as "Randolph." On writing to the Association for Services to Children of the American Library Association, I found that somehow in the early 1960s the initial *J* had crept into their records. They assure me that in the future it shall be corrected.

E. T. B.

The Caldecott Medal

RANDOLPH CALDECOTT AND EDMUND EVANS: A PARTNERSHIP OF EQUALS

BY MICHAEL HUTCHINS

Today when an illustrator produces a picture book for children, his artwork is placed before the impartial eye of the camera and the result is as close to the original as photography can make it. A hundred years ago, although photography was used at one stage, the reputation and success of an illustrator was almost entirely dependent on the skill of the hands and eyes of the wood engraver.

Henry Blackburn, the first London editor to publish a sketch by Randolph Caldecott (in *London Society,* February 1871), and who later became one of his closest friends, saw clearly that an illustrator's work could be ruined by inept or unsympathetic engraving. Writing two years after Caldecott's death, Blackburn thought him more fortunate than most illustrators:

Probably no English artist has benefitted so much by the excellent reproductions of his drawings. He found out the secret very early in his career that the true way to work for reproduction was to be in sympathy with the engraver and colour printer.[1]

In London during the 1870s and 1880s there was a small army of reproductive engravers who could competently copy a pen and ink drawing. But of the masters of the craft, men who could translate the colors and the washes of a watercolor painting into the incised lines of a set of wood engravings, there were but

a few. Of these men the most skilled was Edmund Evans—the man who engraved and printed Randolph Caldecott's *Picture Books*.

The success—artistic, financial, and technical—that Caldecott and Evans achieved was doubtless due to their independence within their partnership. Evans was not contracted by a publisher to produce a picture book; he chose to do so. Caldecott was not employed by Evans to deliver illustrations for a set title: "He was to choose his own subjects and deal with them as his fancy dictated."[2] It was an ideal situation that produced these best-remembered children's books.

Early in 1878 Evans, much impressed by Caldecott's illustrations for Washington Irving's *Bracebridge Hall* and *Old Christmas,* called at the artist's rooms at Great Russell Street and proposed that together they should produce some colored picture books for children. At this time Caldecott's only experience with color engraving and printing had been gained when he was working on two pages in the *Graphic* Christmas number for 1876. There he told the story of the "Christmas Visitors, From My Grandfather's Sketches," nine illustrations close in feeling and characterization to some of his pictures in *Bracebridge Hall.*

Evans speculated on the picture-book project, and Caldecott agreed to make the illustrations for a royalty of three farthings a copy—six and a quarter percent of the shilling that the books cost. Little wonder that he complained, "I get a small royalty—a small, small royalty."[3]

Thirty thousand copies each of *John Gilpin* and *The House that Jack Built* were delivered for Christmas, 1878; by July 1879, sixty thousand had been sold —the small, small royalty had brought him 375 pounds in six months. The percentage was not raised until 1881 for *The Queen of Hearts* and *The Farmer's Boy,* for which he received a penny farthing. But two years later, for *The Fox Jumps over the Parson's Gate* and *A Frog he would a-wooing go,* it was raised again, to three halfpence—twelve and a half percent.

The income from his picture books, which he and later his widow received in the ten years from 1878, was something over 3,400 pounds. There is no simple equation that will bring this sum into present-day figures, but it should probably be multiplied between ten and fifteen times.

Having agreed initially with Evans to undertake two picture books, Caldecott chose his titles and set to work. He first made a blank book of the right size and number of pages and planned what text and illustration would fall on each page. Once he was happy with this rough layout of the book, he began to draw. All his life Caldecott drew spontaneously. He would not labor over a faulty illustration, correcting detail after detail until it satisfied him. The sketch was right when he drew it first or it was thrown aside or given to friends: "This is an important letter so I pack it with some rough protective stuff."[4]

By the middle of August 1878 Caldecott was finishing his picture-book drawings, probably working out the color illustrations, before sending them to be engraved by Evans's skilled workmen.

In 1826, when Edmund Evans was born, Thomas Bewick, the artistic and technical innovator who established wood engraving as the chief medium of book illustration during the nineteenth century, was

seventy-three years old and still had two years to live. During the seven years of an appenticeship with Ebenezer Landells ("Old Tooch-it-oop" who had been a favorite apprentice of Bewick's) the young Edmund acquired the skills that were to make him the best engraver and printer of colored book illustrations in his day.

When he became his own master, the basis of commercial wood engraving had long been established. As early as 1822, William Savage had published *Practical Hints on Decorative Printing,* in which the complexities of color printing from wood blocks were examined in detail for the first time. Landells, Joseph Swain, James Cooper, and others had already realized that it was

Impossible to make any money by sticking to the bench and graver and trying to engrave each block which he engages to do with his own hand.[5]

They, as Evans would in his turn, had begun to commission artists and contract publishers to distribute books in which they—the engraver-printers—had the major interest.

The long years of apprenticeship over, Evans worked solely as an engraver for about four years until in 1851

I started my first handpress next door to the "Old Cheshire Cheese" [perhaps the most famous of all London's public houses] a house a little way up Wine Office Court, at right angles to the "Cheshire Cheese": but soon I received notice to quit, for my pressman had to work early and late and utterly disturbed a quiet lawyer who had his rooms below me. However, my brother found suitable rooms to let at 4 Racquet Court, Fleet Street [the next court to the east, nearer St. Paul's]. Shortly after this we got the whole house and two or three more handpresses to our office.[6]

Evans remained at Racquet Court all his working life. As his business grew, he acquired

The assistance of sundry youths whom he has educated in his own style [until] they have become accomplished engravers.... Then he ... has bought certain machines and engaged accomplished workmen to take off the impressions from the blocks, and further to produce such letterpress [text matter] as may be wanted to accompany the cuts. He has also secured the services of bookbinders ... in short, he has prepared himself to get out and produce in its completeness an illustrated book—plain or in colors.[7]

Later he also took 116 and 119 Fleet Street, which were close to the entrance of Racquet Court.

In addition to his own undoubted skill as an engraver, Evans's success can be attributed to his abilities as a businessman. He fully understood the production processes and he selected his workmen with care.

He could instruct, as Caldecott has written above, apprentices to work in his own style and he made sure that they worked to the high standards he set.

From his apprenticeship he possessed sufficient knowledge of engraving and, in those early years at Racquet Court, taught himself enough about ink mixing and printing to be able to simplify the production of colored illustrations. George Baxter, perhaps the best-known of early color printers, needed to use up to twenty colors a plate, and Savage would print any number from four to fourteen. In his first colored illustrations Evans used just three colors. Certainly in later books he needed more colors than this, but it shows that from the start Evans worked to keep his production costs down.

Third, and here Evans has no equal, he had the ability to choose newcomers—Walter Crane and Kate Greenaway—or an established illustrator unused to working in color—Caldecott—and work with them to produce best-selling titles.

There are now no records of how large an engraving and printing house Evans controlled when he printed Caldecott's books. His grandson thought that during the 1860s and 1870s he probably employed as many as thirty engravers. But just as Evans as a young man saw the rise of reproductive wood engraving (and that his career was central to the success of color printing from wood engravings), so as an old man he saw its decline. The craft for which he had done so much gave way completely to the photographically prepared process plate. He even said about his firm, which for thirty years had produced some of the finest color engraving and printing in England:

Engraving has had its day. I used to employ two rooms of engraving assistants at one time, now they [his sons] can scarcely keep the engraver employed.[8]

Wood engraving was killed by the progressive application of photographic processes. At first, like most new techniques, it was a useful adjunct to an established craft. For five decades before its introduction, the artist drew his illustration directly on the boxwood block. On the comparatively rare occasions when this was impossible, when the artist was particularly famous or was perhaps the special correspondent of a magazine working in Africa or India, then he would draw, as normal, on paper and his work would be redrawn on boxwood by an employee of the engravers. Less-favored would-be illustrators had to learn the techniques of drawing on the unnaturally hard and shiny surface of boxwood, and they were not always successful:

I sent one block to Swain who returned it as too sketchy and asked me to try again. I did so; he sent me the blocks for the other scenes.[9]

Slowly, but increasingly from the 1850s new methods gained popularity, the artist's drawing on paper was photographed and a negative was printed onto boxwood coated with a photographic emulsion. But, even in the 1870s, it was still common to draw directly on the wood.

BROWN OR KEY PLATE

RED

BLUE

PINK

YELLOW

GRAY

Reduced illustrations of the impressions of the six wood block plates used to create the finished print on the facing page

Evans used photography to transfer Caldecott's single-color drawings on boxwood, but in his *Reminiscences* writes that the outline drawings for the colored illustrations were drawn on the wood.[10] However, there is some doubt about this. Evans was writing almost twenty years later, had already suffered one stroke before setting down his memories, and his recollection of this aspect of Caldecott's working methods may well be faulty.

Certainly there were drawings of the colored illustrations. As Beatrix Potter recalled:

Papa [Rupert Potter] went to the Fine Arts Gallery and bought two small pen and ink sketches from Caldecott's Frog [he would a-wooing go]. *He wanted to buy the last colored sketch from the* Fox [Jumps over the Parson's Gate] *but they would not sell it separately.*[11]

Caldecott was not the man to copy colored illustrations speculatively in the hope of some extra income. After this first couple of years in London he was never short of work; bedeviled throughout his life by illness, commissions piled up:

I have a large quantity of work promised to be done between now and next August and I have had to give up [for] the present carrying out some drawings which have been expected any time during the last few months.[12]

When one book was finished, Caldecott's schedule required that he begin his next. There was no time for him to copy work already done.

Once the lines of the illustration were on the boxwood—whether drawn in ink or photographed—the surface was cut away to leave the printing lines higher than the nonprinting areas. Box is a hard, close-grained wood, but after the craftsman had mastered his engraving tool, there was nothing in the single-color illustrations that would give him particular trouble.

The workmen at Racquet Court were *reproductive* engravers. It was their task to reproduce whatever drawing was set before them. Caldecott drew the single-color illustrations and the outlines for the color pages with pen and brown ink, and these were engraved with little trouble in almost frighteningly perfect facsimile.

Colored illustrations were, of course, far more complicated to produce. Caldecott drew the outline—in printers' parlance, the key block—and Evans had this engraved. Proofs of the key block were taken on drawing paper and sent to Caldecott, who colored them and commented where necessary on the standard of engraving.

While he was doing this, Evans's workmen were making "transfers." Several prints of the key block were made and, while the ink on them was still wet, were placed inkside down onto other boxwood blocks. Paper and block were pressed together, almost certainly on an iron hand press, and the ink transferred from the paper to the face of the boxwood. In this way the engraver could place precisely the various colored parts of the illustration.

If an unlimited number of colors could have been used, then an engraver would have cut away in the Japanese fashion all but a smooth, flat area for each separate color. But Evans was not printing in the fifty or sixty colors that Hokusai used. He printed Caldecott's picture books in six: pink, red, blue, yellow, gray, and brown. Yet the skill of Evans and his workmen was such that at no time are we conscious of a limited palette.

A strong magnifying glass will show one green to be made from a solid yellow and narrow lines of blue, a second to be made by printing both blue and yellow in narrow lines, while a third has a fine gray tint added to the blue and yellow. This range of tone and hue, achieved by printing one color upon another, can be seen a dozen times over in every color illustration.

The agreed-upon method of working, that Caldecott should color a proof on cartridge paper with watercolor, meant that the engraver not only had to match the coloring but also had to translate the soft wash gradations into textures that could only be produced by the hard, incised lines of engraving tools. Of these tools there are a basic half dozen, though each is available in four or five widths. Four tools are used to engrave—strictly speaking, to cut lines or dots into the surface of the boxwood—and two are used to clear away larger areas.

The tools used to engrave are the graver, or burin, a diamond-headed tool; the spitsticker, which has a profile like that of a deep-draughted hull of a ship; the tint-tool, with a cuneiform silhouette; and the multiple-tool, which with one stroke gives a number of closely packed parallel lines.

Textures are made by hatching or stippling. In the conventions that were accepted by the commercial wood engraver of the time, hatchings were lines of white that could be parallel and of a constant depth. Cross-hatchings produce diamonds of solid color bounded by white. To create a stipple, the tool is pushed at a high angle just a short way into and along the surface; gravers will give small triangles of white; spitstickers give pear-drop shapes. Criblé is produced when the graver or spitsticker is pushed vertically quite hard into the block and then turned completely.

With just this limited number of tools the range of textures that can be produced by an experienced engraver is almost limitless, but perhaps no wider range is to be seen than in Caldecott's picture books.

Newcomers to the color illustrations will quickly see that most of them are made up of incised lines, but in parts of *John Gilpin* and *Sing a Song for Sixpence,* and throughout *Come Lasses and Lads* and *Ride a Cock Horse* and *A Farmer Went Trotting,* Caldecott's work provided such a challenge that the engraver was forced to create a new range of textures so alien to wood engraving that one authority on children's book illustration has claimed that they were printed lithographically.[13]

Having matched Caldecott's colors and washes, Evans also achieved what was unusual in color printing of the time: a matte finish to his work.

Every nineteenth-century European color printer worked in a similar way, printing at times one color on another. The basic medium of a printing ink is oil, and when two or more colors are overprinted, the result can be varnished, oily, almost lumpy colors. There is none of this in Caldecott's books. Evans chose his inks with uncommon care, and the colors in the picture books are as matte as the watercolors Caldecott made for Evans's guidance.

Contrary to the usual practice of the day, Evans printed the picture books directly from the boxwood. Normally, electrotype printing plates were made to prevent damage to the original engravings, but it is only in recent years that some of the Caldecott illustrations have been electrotyped. While it is probable that much of the detail in the color blocks was too fine to produce satisfactory molds for electrodeposition, there was no reason why the key blocks should not have been electrotyped.

Evans wrote that "the sale of the Toy Books increased so that I printed 100,000 first edition."[14] But this is contradicted by sales figures that Alfred Caldecott, Randolph's younger brother, compiled in 1889. The most popular title, *John Gilpin,* had taken ten years to sell 112,000 copies, and most titles were selling between 6,000 and 7,000 copies each year. Whichever figures one accepts, the books by any standard were a commercial success. But it was this very success that in time rankled.

From the start, Caldecott was not truly satisfied with the royalties he received, and although they were eventually doubled, he thought that the publisher profited disproportionately when his work was compared with that of the engraver and illustrator. An illustration on this theme, "The Profits of a Book," showing a "fat well-to-do publisher with his bag of gold [and] the author, artist and engraver [having] just received their portion,"[15] was censored by Evans when he came to engrave and print *A Sketchbook of R. Caldecott's*.

After only two years, Caldecott thought that, if he were to make more money, the limp-covered shilling books would have to give way to hard-backed florin copies, but the basic 32-page limp format was kept throughout the series. If he had had his way there would have been no picture books produced after 1884. Caldecott had to be persuaded to illustrate *Mrs. Mary Blaize* and *The Great Panjandrum Himself*. And, as they were not published until he had left for America on that last trip to follow the winter sun, it is likely that he did not see printed copies before his death at St. Augustine, Florida, on February 13, 1886.

Had Caldecott not died at the early age of forty, the books that he and Evans would have brought out after 1886 would have been very different—more extensive and more expensive than the picture books. We shall never know what was in his mind when he wrote Evans:

I have an idea of another single book at 2s 6d or so which might be successful. Books of several shillings seem to have difficulty in finding many customers in England. America is the place to publish more expensive books in.[16]

We can only be thankful for those eight years when the reproduction of wood-engraved colored illustrations was at a peak and when sixteen of the best-loved children's books were produced by Randolph Caldecott and Edmund Evans in a unique partnership of equals.

FOOTNOTES

1. Henry Blackburn, *A Memoir of Randolph Caldecott*. Sampson Low, Marston, London, 1887, p. 5.

2. *Pall Mall Gazette,* February 16, 1886.

3. Letter to William Clough, December 13, 1878, in *The Letters of Randolph Caldecott,* edited by Michael Hutchins. Frederick Warne & Company, London and New York, 1974.

4. Letter to William Clough, August 22, 1882, *op. cit.*

5. Letter to Juliana Horatia Ewing, October 18, 1883, *op. cit.*

6. Edmund Evans, *The Reminiscences of Edmund Evans,* edited by Ruari McLean. Oxford University Press, London, 1967, pp. 24–25.

7. Letter to Juliana Horatia Ewing, *op. cit.*

8. Edmund Evans, in a letter dated October 6, 1897, to Mr. Jones.

9. Letter to Thomas Armstrong, June 29, 1871, *op. cit.*

10. Evans, *Reminiscences, op. cit.,* p. 56.

11. *The Journal of Beatrix Potter,* transcribed by Leslie Linder. Frederick Warne & Company, London and New York, 1966.

12. Letter to Juliana Horatia Ewing, December 4, 1881, *op. cit.*

13. Helen Gentry, *Illustrators of Children's Books, 1744–1945*. Boston, 1946, p. 116.

14. Evans, *Reminiscences, op. cit.,* p. 59.

15. Edmund Evans, in a letter dated October 16, 1897, to Mr. Jones.

16. Letter to Edmund Evans, November 5, 1884, *op. cit.*

SELECTIONS FROM THE WORK OF RANDOLPH CALDECOTT

EARLY SKETCHES

The earliest of the sketches reproduced here were made when Caldecott was employed at the Manchester and Salford Bank in Manchester between 1867 and 1872.

Caldecott's occupation as a bank clerk is always referred to with pride. We forget that, in truth, the work was uninspiring. As an escape from the tedium of copying or adding long columns of figures, Caldecott sketched on scraps of paper which were handy—a habit carried over from his school days. He was not concerned with line or style, only in amusing himself and fellow employees.

When Caldecott made the move to London, he strolled through the dirty, noisy streets of the city recording scenes new to him. The first year, although exciting, was at times lonely and discouraging. For the first time in his life Caldecott lived and worked alone. He greatly missed the companionship of his fellow bank clerks—people from a similar background. A feeling of dispiritedness comes through in sketches he made on letters to friends.

A study of this group of sketches reveals his difficulties as an artist as well as the variety of styles he explored in his early career.

*Sketch and poem
on notepaper of
the Manchester
and Salford Bank*

When first we met
'Twas in the wet
We sat upon a stile.
Oh, happy hours
In falling showers!
You squeezed me all the
while

MANCHESTER

MANCHESTER AND SALFORD BANK.

V. A. M.

E.3679-1927

70

V. A. M.

E 3687 - 1927

V. A. M.

James Blower

E 3689 - 1927

V. A. M.

E.3688 - 1924

V. A. M.

E. 3687 - 1927

V. A. M.

E.3691 - 1924

V. A. M.

E.3690 - 1927

Fellow employees at the Manchester and Salford Bank with their names on scraps of paper

Early Manchester works. Caldecott appears (second from left) *in picture at left*

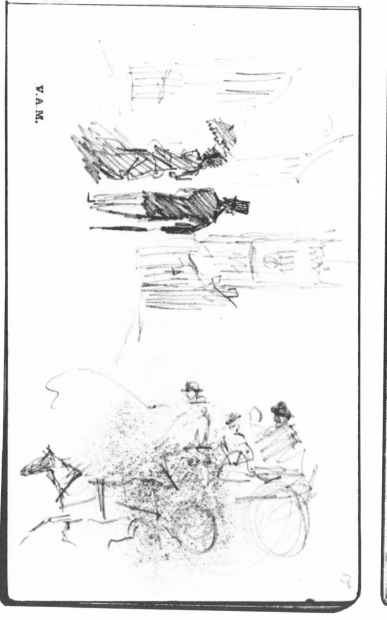

These sketches and those on p. 74 were made in the first small sketch book
Caldecott used when he went to London to study and become an artist

£ 3671 - 1927

V. A. M.
1870

Whitchurch by Realdicott

This is R.C. when he feels as though he was going to take to drink.
(N.B. he very often feels so)

V. A. M.   £ 3686 - 1927
*Caldecott's first attempt at
drawing for wood cutting*

Hunting in the Midlands. Possibly executed as studies for bas relief

Dressed up lad on a pony

A boy studies Latin while scaring crows from the corn with a clapper

Caldecott bows courteously as an artist beginning a new life

Sketched when he visited Rotten Row, Hyde Park, London

Sketched when he visited Rotten Row, Hyde Park, London

80

More impressions of London showing Caldecott's ability to caricature

First picture to appear in Punch,
Volume 62, June 22, 1872

Henry Irving as Hamlet

The speaker going to the House of Lords

SKETCHES MADE WHEN VISITING PARLIAMENT

The Prime Minister delivers his address

*At the bar in the
House of Lords*

The arrival of new members to the House of Commons

*The last day of the long
Tichborne Trial 1874*

84

EUROPEAN SKETCHES

When Caldecott lived in London, his talent was nurtured by Thomas Armstrong and Henry Blackburn. It was Blackburn who first suggested Caldecott go to Europe to sketch and also to broaden his outlook on life and gain social experience.

The drawings, made over a period of years, serve to show Caldecott's development. Whether portraying people in the Harz Mountains, Brittany, or Italy, they show Caldecott's ability to capture tender feelings as well as humor. The country people attracted him most, probably because these were the kind of people he could best relate to from his own background.

In a variety of moods these pictures represent a wide range of styles. Caldecott continued his early habit of including himself in some of the scenes.

**STUDIES OF PEOPLE
IN THE HARZ MOUNTAINS**

A peasant woman of the Harz Mountains

*A visit to Brocken. Caldecott's
lank figure is on the left*

Drinking the mineral waters at Goslar

Riding the tram car to the Universal Exhibition of Arts and Industry, Vienna, 1873

A study of the variety of caps in Brittany

Going to market in Carhaix

The Ronde, a country dance

*Caldecott portrays himself
sketching under difficulties*

A betrothal party at an old inn in Guemene

On the roadside near Brest

Chateauneuf du Faou, the wandering minstrels

The husbandman
from North Italian Folk

The priest and the player, Italy

*Women gossiping,
Italy*

Caldecott (on left) watching the gambling at Monte Carlo

A sketch of Caldecott returning from work at Pont Aven, 1878

AMERICAN SKETCHES

These nine drawings and the accompanying text comprised the two parts of "American Facts and Fancies," the opening of the incompleted series for which the *Graphic* had commissioned Caldecott before he embarked on the journey to the United States.

The editor of the *Graphic* wished Caldecott to record the sights as well as the American way of life while traveling extensively throughout the United States.

Caldecott's text and pictures record a rough Atlantic crossing sailing on the northern route out of Liverpool on the Cunard ship *Aurania*. They provide an amusing view of travel at that time. His impressions of life in the United States impart a feeling of an era long gone.

The articles appeared in the *Graphic*, February through June 1886.

ON THE WAY OUT—"A BIG STEAMER LIKE THIS NEVER ROLLS"

The first two pictures explain themselves. Everyone who has made a sea voyage knows that steamers can roll, however big they may be, and can recall the lively appearance at such a time of a cabin interior, with everything movable swaying to and fro

ON THE WAY OUT—EFFECT PRODUCED BY A ROUGH NIGHT
ON GARMENTS HANGING UP IN ONE'S STATEROOM

AT NEW YORK: READY TO LAND—YOUNG AMERICAN
RETURNING FROM HIS TRAVELS IN EUROPE

"At New York ready to land." *The picture on right depicts a very youthful and diminutive citizen of the United States, who looks as if he had not long quitted the nursery, but who has, nevertheless, been doing the grand European tour all by himself, unattended and alone*

AT WASHINGTON—COUNTRY PEOPLE IN THE ROTUNDA OF THE CAPITOL

"At Washington" *is thus described by Mr. Caldecott:*

The Capitol at Washington was dull during my visit; there were no statesmen or lobbyists, only a few country people looking at the Chambers, and at the historical pictures in the Rotunda. Some of these great pictures represent the humiliation of various British generals, one shows the baptism of Pocahontas, and another the Declaration of Independence. The last is indicated in the accompanying sketch, and is interesting because of the careful portraits. It is a very fair specimen of this kind of work. John Randolph, during a debate in Congress, called it the "shin-piece," because of the abundance of legs displayed in it.

A YANKEE IN A
STREET CAR, PHILADELPHIA

A BRACE OF
WASHINGTON POLITICIANS

PENNSYLVANIA AVENUE, WASHINGTON

As the period of my arrival was not during the Session of Congress, there were few statesmen to be seen walking about, but the fatigue of a little exploratory tour was rewarded by the discovery of a smoking politician or two preparing for the coming campaign.

At Philadelphia I was shocked by the lavish display of shop-signs and other street advertisements, and bewildered by the cobweb of telegraph wires and the forests of poles in the chief streets. There are some very clean streets of comfortable looking red houses with white doors, white or grey-green shutters, and

well-kept steps; but the tram cars (in one of which my sketch of the Yankee was taken) and horse-railways run along these streets as well as along the business thoroughfares, and produce an effect of incongruity and a lack of repose.

Washington, which used to be called "The City of Magnificent Distances," is now a fine town with imposing public buildings, and wide, clean streets. The larger of these are called Avenues. The view along Pennsylvania Avenue either way, towards the

SCENE IN A HOTEL, WASHINGTON

Capitol or towards the White House, is something of which an American can be justly proud although a closer inspection shows that many of the buildings in the Avenue are mean.

On arriving at my hotel at Washington, I had the first good broad effect of negros. A crowd of dark grinning porters, with shirts over other garments, received the omnibus. In the hall of the hotel men of a lighter shade in black jackets passed the guests into the reception room, and still paler gentlemen in longer coats introduced us to white clerks in the office. The large dining or coffee-room was white and bright, the white covered tables were many and the waiters were all colored. A head-waiter of medium tint, with hair, whiskers, and moustache carefully dressed, showed new-comers to their seats with a slow studied wave of the hand.

FOX-HUNTING IN AMERICA—A FANCY

The most prominent features of the landscape as seen from the train between New York and Washington are the huge advertisements in white letters painted upon black wooden barns and work-shops, and upon black hoardings specially set up in the fields within view of the railway, but not close to the line. I hear that even natural rocks are made to bear these marks of commercial enterprise.

As I was told that there are plenty of packs of foxhounds in the Eastern States, I could not help having a vision of a hunting scene, and I here give a sketch of it as it appeared to my mind's eye.

Negroes loading cotton bales in Charleston. Last drawing ever made by Randolph Caldecott 1885

104

BARON BRUNO

Selections from *Baron Bruno; or, The Unbelieving Philosopher, and other Fairy Stories,* by Louisa Morgan. This was one of Caldecott's first books for children. It was published by Macmillan and Company in London in 1875.

It is of interest because the illustrations disclose Caldecott's lack of freedom as an illustrator. The drawings are detailed to the point of being overfinished, as was the custom of the time. Only in the illustration of Fidunia feeding the geese does one capture a feeling of motion and excitement in the hungry goslings.

Certainly the illustrations do not hint at the joy and movement which would burst forth when Caldecott illustrated old rhymes more familiar to him.

BARON BRUNO:

OR,

THE UNBELIEVING PHILOSOPHER,

And other Fairy Stories.

BY

LOUISA MORGAN.

WITH ILLUSTRATIONS BY R. CALDECOTT.

London:
MACMILLAN AND CO.
1875.

OLD CHRISTMAS

Old Christmas, from the Sketch Book of Washington Irving, was published in December of 1875 by Macmillan and Company of London.

The one hundred and twenty drawings were made in 1874. Caldecott had received his first artistic instruction only seven years earlier. He had only two years of professional work behind him when he undertook this task.

Study of the illustrations shows that while working, Caldecott abandoned his gift of caricature. He developed into an artist and illustrator whose pictures unfold more of the story than the text reveals.

James D. Cooper, who called himself the old woodpecker, was one of the outstanding wood engravers of all time. He worked during 1875 engraving the drawings most faithfully on wood.

OLD CHRISTMAS:

FROM THE Sketch Book of Washington Irving.

ILLUSTRATED BY R. CALDECOTT

London.
Macmillan & Co

1882

A man might then behold
  At Christmas, in each hall
Good fires to curb the cold,
  And meat for great and small.
The neighbours were friendly bidden,
  And all had welcome true,
The poor from the gates were not chidden,
  When this old cap was new.

OLD SONG.

110

BRACEBRIDGE HALL

Bracebridge Hall, by Washington Irving, was published in December of 1876 by Macmillan and Company of London. Caldecott made the one hundred and sixteen drawings for the work during the first half of that year. He had settled down to work as a professional.

The wood engraving was once more executed by James D. Cooper. Although similar to *Old Christmas* and equally well received, this work never gained the popularity of *Old Christmas*.

Caldecott executed the cover design for both *Old Christmas* and *Bracebridge Hall,* a habit he was to continue when he illustrated the *Picture Books*.

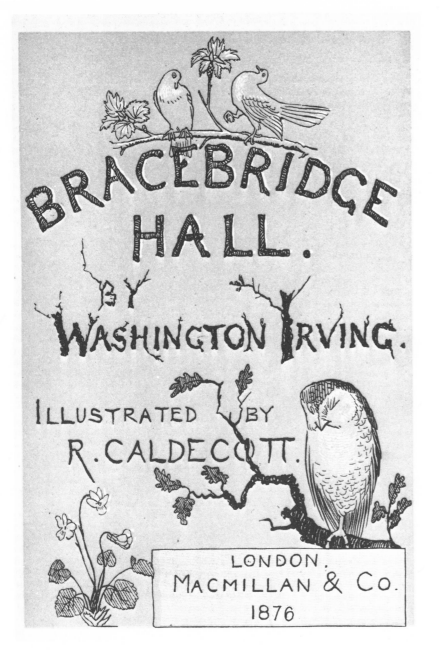

BRACEBRIDGE HALL.

BY

WASHINGTON IRVING.

ILLUSTRATED BY

R. CALDECOTT.

LONDON.
MACMILLAN & Co.
1876

A Literary Antiquary.

126

SELECTIONS
FROM OTHER BOOKS

In January of 1873 Caldecott made six full-page black-and-white illustrations for *Frank Mildmay or The Naval Officer,* by Captain Marryat, who was the author of the earliest of the historical adventure stories written especially for children. Captain Marryat had died twenty-five years earlier and the book contained a Memoir by Florence Marryat. It is probably the first book Caldecott illustrated for children. The pictures were engraved by Edmund Evans and it was published by George Routledge and Sons.

Caldecott provided illustrations for a number of books written by Edwin Waugh, the well-known, versatile writer from Lancashire. It was Waugh who adapted the old Lancashire rhyme *Old Cronies* and published it as *The Three Jolly Hunters.* Caldecott, on reading Waugh's version, made a few changes, wrote an additional verse, added his lively illustrations, and published it as *The Three Jovial Huntsmen* in 1880.

For Juliana H. Ewing, Caldecott illustrated *Daddy Darwin's Dovecote* and *Lob Lie-by-the-Fire* as well as *Jackanapes.* All were published by the Society for Promoting Christian Knowledge.

The blackbird on a small white hillock. One of four illustrations made by Caldecott for What the Blackbird Said: A Story in Four Chirps, *by Mrs. Frederick Locker, published in London and New York in 1881 by George Routledge and Sons*

130

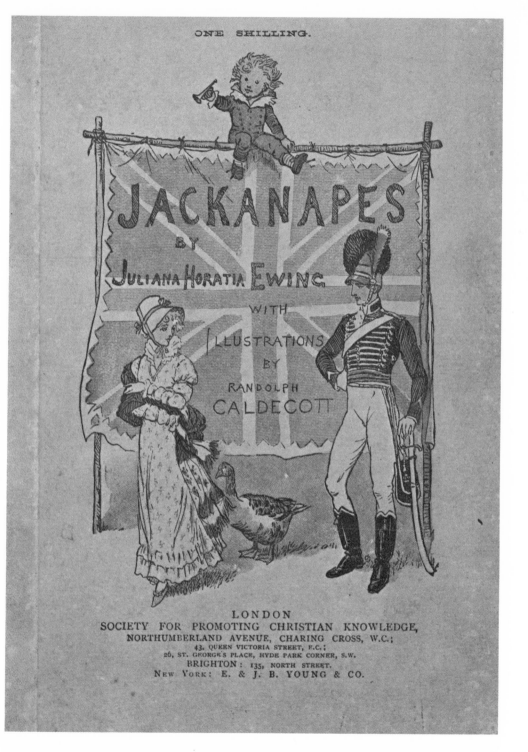

Cover of Jackanapes *designed by Caldecott. Juliana Horatia Ewing and Caldecott collaborated closely on this book and two later stories*

131

From Jack and the Beanstalk. English Hexameters, *by Hallam Tennyson, son of Alfred, Lord Tennyson. This work was published by Macmillan and Company after Caldecott's death in 1886 and illustrated with Caldecott's first rough sketches*

SELECTIONS FROM AESOP'S FABLES

These drawings are from *Some of Aesop's Fables with Modern Instances* from new translations by Alfred Caldecott, published in 1883 by Macmillan and Company. Caldecott's younger brother made the translations and James D. Cooper the engravings. The modern instances provided an interpretation of the old fable for the society of Caldecott's time. Caldecott appears in many of the sketches.

SOME OF

ÆSOP'S FABLES

WITH

MODERN INSTANCES

SHEWN IN DESIGNS

BY

RANDOLPH CALDECOTT

FROM NEW TRANSLATIONS BY ALFRED CALDECOTT, M.A.

THE ENGRAVINGS BY J. D. COOPER

London

MACMILLAN AND CO.

1883

The title page

Drawing facing the opening text page

134

A certain Coppersmith had a Puppy. While the Coppersmith was at work the Puppy lay asleep; but when mealtime came he woke up. So his master, throwing him a bone, said: "You sleepy little wretch of a Puppy, what shall I do with you, you inveterate sluggard? When I am thumping on my anvil you can go to sleep on the mat; but when I come to work my teeth immediately you are wide awake and wagging your tail at me."

THE COPPERSMITH AND HIS PUPPY

THE FOX WITHOUT A TAIL

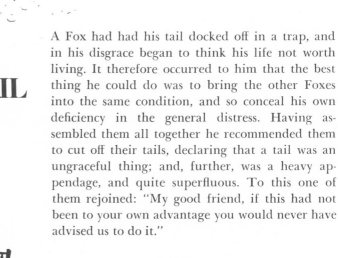

A Fox had had his tail docked off in a trap, and in his disgrace began to think his life not worth living. It therefore occurred to him that the best thing he could do was to bring the other Foxes into the same condition, and so conceal his own deficiency in the general distress. Having assembled them all together he recommended them to cut off their tails, declaring that a tail was an ungraceful thing; and, further, was a heavy appendage, and quite superfluous. To this one of them rejoined: "My good friend, if this had not been to your own advantage you would never have advised us to do it."

"Nonsense, my dears! Husbands are ridiculous things & are quite unnecessary!"

The Lion one day went out hunting along with three other Beasts, and they caught a Stag. With the consent of the others the Lion divided it, and he cut it into four equal portions; but when the others were going to take hold of their shares, "Gently, my friends," said the Lion; "the first of these portions is mine, as one of the party; the second also is mine, because of my rank among beasts; the third you will yield me as a tribute to my courage and nobleness of character; while, as to the fourth,—why, if any one wishes to dispute with me for it, let him begin, and we shall soon see whose it will be."

THE LION AND OTHER BEASTS

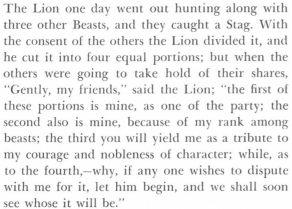

THE DOG AND THE WOLF

A Wolf, seeing a large Dog with a collar on, asked him: "Who put that collar round your neck, and fed you to be so sleek?" "My master," answered the Dog. "Then," said the Wolf, "may no friend of mine be treated like this; a collar is as grievous as starvation."

A selection of other illustrations from
Some of Aesop's Fables with Modern Instances

Additional illustrations from Aesop's Fables

SELECTIONS FROM MAGAZINE ARTICLES

Caldecott's first published work appeared in the *Illustrated London News,* December 7, 1861. It was not until he went to live and work in Manchester seven years later that he had another drawing published. The *Will o' The Wisp* and *The Sphinx,* two short-lived newspapers published while Caldecott lived in Manchester, both used his sketches.

In London his drawings appeared in *Belgravia, A London Magazine, London Society, The Pictorial World, Punch, The Graphic,* and *English Illustrated Magazine.* His work also appeared in *Aunt Judy's Magazine* at the request of Mrs. Ewing and her sister Mrs. Gatty, who was the editor.

In the United States of America his work appeared in *Harper's New Monthly Magazine* and the *New York Daily Graphic.*

The Spectators.

These two illustrations were used in the February 1883 issue of Aunt Judy's
Magazine *to illustrate a story by Mrs. Ewing, "Mother's Birthday Review." They
also appear in* A Sketchbook of R. Caldecott's, *which was published by George
Routledge and Sons in 1883*

142

Review of the Household Troops.

The Cavalry.

R.C.

THE CHARACTER OF DOGS

This article is of interest because it brings together Robert Louis Stevenson and Randolph Caldecott. When Stevenson wrote *Treasure Island* he let his enthusiasm sweep the story along, filling it with excitement, speed, and color. In doing this, he left behind all the moral attitudes other writers for children had felt it proper to preserve.

Caldecott let his enthusiasm carry him along when he illustrated the *Picture Books*. Action and humor filled the pages, leaving behind rules set by earlier illustrators. Strangely enough, none of this tremendous change is evident in this piece.

This article appeared in *English Illustrated Magazine,* February 1884.

THE CHARACTER OF DOGS.

THE civilisation, the manners and the morals of dog-kind are to a great extent subordinated to those of his ancestral master, man. This animal, in many ways so superior, has accepted a position of inferiority, shares the domestic life, and humours the caprices of the tyrant. But the potentate, like the British in India, pays small regard to the character of his willing client, judges him with listless glances, and condemns him in a bye-word. Listless have been the looks of his admirers, who have exhausted idle terms of praise, and buried the poor soul below exaggerations. And yet more idle and, if possible, more unintelligent has been the attitude of his express detractors: those who are very fond of dogs "but in their proper place;" who say "poo' fellow, poo' fellow," and are themselves far poorer; who whet the knife of the vivisectionist or heat his oven; who are not ashamed to admire "the creature's instinct;" and flying far beyond folly, have dared to resuscitate the theory of animal machines. The "dog's instinct" and the "automaton-dog," in this age of psychology and science, sound like strange anachronisms. An automaton, he certainly is: a machine working independently of his control, the heart like the mill-wheel, keeping all in motion, and the consciousness, like a person shut in the mill garret, enjoying the view out of the window

and shaken by the thunder of the stones:— an automaton in one corner of which a living spirit is confined: an automaton like man. Instinct again, he certainly possesses. Inherited aptitudes are his, inherited frailties. Some things he at once views and understands, as though he were awakened from a sleep, as though he came "trailing clouds of glory." But with him, as with man, the field of instinct is limited; its utterances are obscure and occasional; and about the far larger part of life both the dog and his master must conduct their steps by deduction and observation.

The leading distinction between dog and man, after and perhaps before the different duration of their lives, is that the one can speak and that the other cannot. The absence of the power of speech confines the dog in the development of his intellect; it hinders him from many speculations, for words are the beginning of metaphysic; at the same blow it saves him from many superstitions; and his silence has won for him a higher name for virtue than his conduct justifies. The faults of the dog are many. He is vainer than man, singularly greedy of notice, singularly intolerant of ridicule, suspicious like the deaf, jealous to the degree of frenzy, and radically devoid of truth. The day of an intelligent small dog is passed in the manufacture and the laborious communication of falsehood; he lies with his tail, he lies with his eye, he lies with his protesting paw; and when he rattles his dish or scratches at the door his purpose is other than appears. But he has some apology to offer for the vice. Many of the signs which form his dialect have come to bear an arbitrary meaning, clearly understood both by his master and himself; yet when a new want arises he must either invent a new vehicle of meaning or wrest an old one to a different purpose; and this necessity,

frequently recurring, must tend to lessen his idea of the sanctity of symbols. Meanwhile the dog is clear in his own conscience, and draws, with a human nicety, the distinction between formal and essential truth. Of his punning perversions, his legitimate dexterity with symbols, he is even vain; but when he has told or been detected in a lie, there is not a hair upon his body but confesses guilt. To a dog of gentlemanly feeling, theft and falsehood are disgraceful vices. The canine, like the human, gentleman demands in his misdemeanours Montaigne's "*je ne sais quoi de généreux.*" He is never more than half ashamed of having barked or bitten; and for those faults into which he has been led by the desire to shine before a lady of his

race, he retains, even under physical correction, a share of pride. But to be caught lying, if he understands it, instantly uncurls his fleece.

Just as among dull observers he preserves a name for truth, the dog has been credited with modesty. It is amazing how the use of language blunts the faculties of man—that because vainglory finds no vent in words, creatures supplied with eyes have been unable to detect a fault so gross and obvious. If a small spoiled dog were suddenly to be endowed with speech, he would prate interminably, and still about himself: when we had friends, we should be forced to lock him in a garret; and what with his whining jealousies and his foible for false-

hood, in a year's time he would have gone far to weary out our love. I was about to compare him to Sir Willoughby Patterne, but the Patternes have a manlier sense of their own merits; and the parallel, besides, is ready. Hans Christian Andersen, as we behold him in his startling memoirs, thrilling from top to toe with an excruciating vanity, and scouting even along the street for shadows of offence—here was the talking dog.

It is just this rage for consideration that has betrayed the dog into his satellite position as the friend of man. The cat, an animal of franker appetites, preserves his independence. But the dog, with one eye ever on the audience, has been wheedled into slavery, and

SOCIAL INEQUALITY.
From a Drawing by RANDOLPH CALDECOTT.

praised and patted into the renunciation of his nature. Once he ceased hunting and became man's plate-licker, the Rubicon was crossed. Thenceforth he was a gentleman of leisure; and except the few whom we keep working, the whole race grew more and more self-conscious, mannered and affected. The number of things that a small dog does naturally is strangely small. Enjoying better spirits and not crushed under material cares, he is far more theatrical than average man. His whole life, if he be a dog of any pretension to gallantry, is spent in a vain show, and in the hot pursuit of admiration. Take out your puppy for a walk, and you will find the little ball of fur clumsy, stupid, bewildered, but natural. Let but a few months pass, and when you repeat the process you will find nature buried in convention. He will do nothing plainly; but the simplest processes of our material life will all be bent into the forms of an elaborate and mysterious etiquette. Instinct, says the fool, has awakened. But it is not so. Some dogs—some, at the very least—if they be kept separate from others, remain quite natural; and these, when at length they meet with a companion of experience, and have the game explained to them, distinguish themselves by the severity of their devotion to its rules. I wish I were allowed to tell a story which would radiantly illuminate the point; but men, like dogs, have an elaborate and mysterious etiquette. It is their bond of sympathy that both are the children of convention.

The Wife-beater.

THE HERO OF A SAD HISTORY.
From a Drawing by RANDOLPH CALDECOTT.

The person, man or dog, who has a conscience is eternally condemned to some degree of humbug; the sense of the law in their members fatally precipitates either towards a frozen and affected bearing. And the converse is true; and in the elaborate and conscious manners of the dog, moral opinions and the love of the ideal stand confessed. To follow for ten minutes in the street some swaggering, canine cavalier, is to receive a lesson in dramatic art and the cultured conduct of the body; in every act and gesture you see him true to a refined conception; and the dullest cur, beholding him, pricks up his ear and proceeds to imitate and parody that charming ease. For to be a high-mannered and high-minded gentleman, careless, affable, and gay, is the inborn pretension of the dog. The large dog, so

much lazier, so much more weighed upon with matter, so majestic in repose, so beautiful in effort, is born with the dramatic means to wholly represent the part. And it is more pathetic and perhaps more instructive to consider the small dog in his conscientious and imperfect efforts to outdo Sir Philip Sidney. For the ideal of the dog is feudal and religious; the ever-present polytheism, the whip-bearing Olympus of mankind, rules them on the one hand; on the other, their singular difference of size and strength among themselves effectually prevents the appearance of the democratic notion. Or we might more exactly compare their society to the curious spectacle presented by a school—ushers, monitors, and big and little boys—qualified by one circumstance, the introduction of the other sex. In each, we should observe a somewhat similar tension of manner, and somewhat similar points of honour. In each, the larger animal keeps a contemptuous good humour; in each the smaller annoys him with wasplike impudence, certain of practical immunity; in each we shall find a double life producing double characters, and an excursive and noisy heroism combined with a fair amount of practical timidity. I have known dogs, and I have known school heroes that, set aside the fur, could hardly have been told apart; and if we desire to understand the chivalry of old, we must turn to the school playfields or the dungheap where the dogs are trooping.

Woman, with the dog, has been long enfranchised. Incessant massacre of female innocents has changed the proportions of the sexes and perverted their relations. Thus, when we regard the manners of the dog, we see a romantic and monogamous animal, once perhaps as delicate as the cat, at war with impossible conditions. Man has much to answer for; and the part he plays is yet more damnable and parlous than Corin's in the eyes of Touchstone. But his intervention has, at least, created an imperial situation for the rare surviving ladies. In that society they reign without a rival: conscious queens; and in the only instance of a canine wife-beater that has ever fallen under my notice, the criminal was somewhat excused by the circumstances of his story. He is a little, very alert, well-bred, intelligent Skye, as black as a hat, with a wet bramble for a nose and two cairngorms for eyes. To the human observer, he is decidedly well-looking; but to the ladies of his race he seems abhorrent. A thorough, elaborate gentleman, of the plume and sword-knot order, he was born

with a nice sense of gallantry to women. He took at their hands the most outrageous treatment; I have heard him bleating like a sheep, I have seen him streaming blood, and his ear tattered like a regimental banner; and yet he would scorn to make reprisals. Nay more, when a human lady upraised the contumelious whip against the very dame who had been so cruelly misusing him, my little great-heart gave but one hoarse cry and fell upon the tyrant, tooth and nail. This is the tale of a soul's tragedy. After three years of unavailing chivalry, he suddenly, in one hour, threw off the yoke of obligation; had he been Shakespeare he would then have written *Troilus and Cressida* to brand the offending sex; but being only a little dog, he began to bite them. The surprise of the ladies whom he attacked indicated the monstrosity of his offence; but he had fairly beaten off his better angel, fairly committed moral suicide; for almost in the same hour, throwing aside the last rags of decency, he proceeded to attack the aged also. The fact is worth remark, showing, as it does, that ethical laws are common both to dogs and men; and that with both a single deliberate violation of the conscience loosens all. "But while the lamp holds on to burn," says the paraphrase, "the greatest sinner may return." I have been cheered to see symptoms of effectual penitence in my sweet ruffian; and by the handling that he accepted uncomplainingly the other day from an indignant fair one, I begin to hope the period of *sturm und drang* is closed.

All these little gentlemen are subtle casuists. The duty to the female dog is plain; but where competing duties rise, down they will sit and study them out, like Jesuit confessors. I knew another little Skye, somewhat plain in manner and appearance, but a creature compact of amiability and solid wisdom. His family going abroad for a winter, he was received for that period by an uncle in the same city. The winter over, his own family home again, and his own house (of which he was very proud) re-opened, he found himself in a dilemma between two conflicting duties of loyalty and gratitude. His old friends were not to be neglected, but it seemed hardly decent to desert the new. This was how he solved the problem. Every morning, as soon as the door was opened, off posted Coolin to his uncle's, visited the children in the nursery, saluted the whole family, and was back at home in time for breakfast and his bit of fish. Nor was this done without a sacrifice on his part, sharply felt; for he had to forego the particular honour

and jewel of his day—his morning's walk with my father. And, perhaps from this cause, he gradually wearied of and relaxed the practice, and at length returned entirely to his ancient habits. But the same decision served him in another and more distressing case of divided duty, which happened not long after. He was not at all a kitchen dog, but the cook had nursed him with unusual kindness during the distemper; and though he did not adore her as he adored my father—although (born snob) he was critically conscious of her position as "only a servant" —he still cherished for her a special gratitude. Well, the cook left, and retired some streets away to lodgings of her own; and there was Coolin in precisely the same situation with any young gentleman who has had the inestimable benefit of a faithful nurse. The canine conscience did not solve the problem with a pound of, tea at Christmas. No longer content to pay a flying visit, it was the whole forenoon that he dedicated to his solitary friend. And so, day by day, he continued to comfort her solitude until (for some reason which I could never understand and cannot approve) he was kept locked up to break him of the graceful habit. Here, it is not the similarity, it is the difference, that is worthy of remark; the clearly marked degrees of gratitude and the proportional duration of his visits. Anything farther removed from instinct it were hard to fancy; and one is even stirred to a certain impatience with a character so destitute of spontaneity, so passionless in justice, and so priggishly obedient to the voice of reason.

There are not many dogs like this good Coolin, and not many people. But the type is one well marked, both in the human and the canine family. Gallantry was not his aim, but a solid and somewhat oppressive respectability. He was a sworn foe to the unusual and the conspicuous, a praiser of the golden mean, a kind of city uncle modified by Cheeryble. And as he was precise and conscientious in all the steps of his own blameless course, he looked for the same precision and an even greater gravity in the bearing of his deity, my father. It was no sinecure to be Coolin's idol: he was exacting like a rigid parent; and at every sign of levity in the man whom he respected, he announced loudly the death of virtue and the proximate fall of the pillars of the earth. I have called him a snob; but all dogs are so, though in varying degrees. It is hard to follow their snobbery among themselves; for though I think we can perceive distinctions of rank, we cannot grasp what is the criterion.

Thus in Edinburgh, in a good part of the town, there were several distinct societies or clubs that met in the morning to—the phrase is technical—to "rake the backets" in a troop. A friend of mine, the master of three dogs, was one day surprised to observe that they had left one club and joined another; but whether it was a rise or a fall, and the result of an invitation or an expulsion, was more than he could guess. And this illustrates pointedly our ignorance of the real life of dogs, their social ambitions and their social hierarchies. At least, in their dealings with men they are not only conscious of sex, but of the difference of station. And that in the most snobbish manner; for

NOT RECEIVED IN SOCIETY.
From a Drawing by RANDOLPH CALDECOTT.

the poor man's dog is not offended by the notice of the rich, and keeps all his ugly feeling for those poorer or more ragged than his master. And again, for every station they have an ideal of behaviour, to which the master, under pain of derogation, will do wisely to conform. How often has not a cold glance of an eye informed me that my dog was disappointed; and how much more gladly would he not have taken a beating than to be thus wounded in the seat of piety!

I knew one disrespectable dog. He was far liker a cat; cared little or nothing for men, with whom he merely co-existed as we do with cattle, and was entirely devoted to the art of poaching. A house would not hold him,

and to live in a town was what he refused. He led, I believe, a life of troubled but genuine pleasure, and perished beyond all question in a trap. But this was an exception, a marked reversion to the ancestral type; like the hairy, human infant. The true dog of the nineteenth century, to judge by the remainder of my fairly large acquaintance, is in love with respectability. A street-dog was once adopted by a lady. While still an Arab, he had done as Arabs do, gambolling in the mud, charging into butchers' stalls, a cat-hunter, a sturdy beggar, a common rogue and vagabond; but with his rise into society, he laid aside these inconsistent pleasures. He stole no more, he hunted no more cats; and conscious of his collar, he ignored his old companions. Yet the canine upper class was never brought to recognise the upstart, and from that hour, except for human countenance, he was alone. Friendless, shorn of his sports and the habits of a lifetime, he still lived in a glory of happiness, content with his acquired respectability, and with no care but to support it solemnly. Are we to condemn or praise this self-made dog? We praise his human brother. And thus to conquer vicious habits is as rare with dogs as with men. With the more part, for all their scruple-mongering and moral thought, the vices that are born with them remain invincible throughout; and they live all their years,

glorying in their virtues, but still the slaves of their defects. Thus the sage Coolin was a thief to the last; among a thousand peccadilloes, a whole goose and a whole cold leg of mutton lay upon his conscience; but Woggs, whose soul's shipwreck in the matter of gallantry I have recounted above, has only twice been known to steal, and has often nobly conquered the temptation. The eighth is his favourite commandment. There is something painfully human in these unequal virtues and mortal frailties of the best. Still more painful is the bearing of those " stammering professors " in the house of sickness and under the terror of death. It is beyond a doubt to me that, somehow or other, the dog connects together, or confounds, the uneasiness of sickness and the consciousness of guilt. To the pains of the body he often adds the tortures of the conscience; and at these times his haggard protestations form, in regard to the human deathbed, a dreadful parody or parallel.

I once supposed that I had found an inverse relation between the double etiquette which dogs obey; and that those who were most addicted to the showy street life among other dogs were less careful in the practice of home virtues for the tyrant man. But the female dog, that mass of carneying affections, shines equally in either sphere; rules her rough posse of attendant swains with unwearying tact and gusto; and with her master and mistress pushes the arts of insinuation to their crowning point. The attention of man and the regard of other dogs flatter (it would thus appear) the same sensibility,

but perhaps, if we could read the canine heart, they would be found to flatter it in very different degrees. Dogs live with man as courtiers round a monarch, steeped in the flattery of his notice and enriched with sinecures. To push their favour in this world of pickings and caresses is, perhaps, the business of their lives; and their joys may lie outside. I am in despair at our persistent ignorance. I read in the lives of our companions the same processes of reason, the same antique and fatal conflicts of the right against the wrong, and of unbitted nature with too rigid custom; I see them with our weaknesses, vain, false, inconstant against appetite, and with our one stalk of virtue, devoted to the dream of an ideal; and yet, as they hurry by me on the street with tail in air, or come singly to solicit my regard, I must own the secret purport of their lives is still inscrutable to man. Is man the friend, or is he the patron only? Have they indeed forgotten nature's voice? or are those moments snatched from courtiership when they touch noses with the tinker's mongrel, the brief reward and pleasure of their artificial lives? Doubtless, when man shares with his dog the toils of a profession and the pleasures of an art, as with the shepherd or the poacher, the affection warms and strengthens till it fills the soul. But doubtless, also, the masters are, in many cases, the object of a merely interested cultus, sitting aloft like Louis Quatorze, giving and receiving flattery and favour; and the dogs, like the majority of men, have but foregone their true existence and become the dupes of their ambition.

ROBERT LOUIS STEVENSON.

THE PRODUCT OF CIVILISATION.
From a Drawing by RANDOLPH CALDECOTT.

Y

FOX HUNTING: BY A MAN IN A ROUND HAT

Fox-Hunting: By a Man in a Round Hat. This article was written and illustrated by Randolph Caldecott. The magazine was edited by J. W. Comyns Carr; his wife, Alice Comyns Carr, was the author of *North Italian Folk: Sketches of Town and Country Life,* published in 1878 by Chatto and Windus with illustrations by Caldecott. This article appeared in *English Illustrated Magazine,* March 1886.

THE MEET

SOME ROUND-HATS. "Truly it is a beautiful sight to see hounds bounding and jumping over a bit of wild land covered with brown heather and dead ferns."

149

AT THE COVERT SIDE. *"Some turn out to sell their horses, and some to show their clothes; but nobody goes out because he believes his help is wanted in destroying a thieving little beast of unpleasant odour."*

GONE AWAY! *"The illustration which I call 'Gone Away!' represents the hounds leaving a patch of gorse and hurrying forward on a breast-high scent . . ."*

ON THE SURREY COMMONS. "... *exhibits a 'whip' (properly called a whipper-in) and a few others getting over one of the usual low banks. They are often rotten and have ditches obscured by heather and ferns.*"

AMONG THE TURNIPS. "*I have known people land on a heap of turnips which have been shot down under the hedge on the far side, and find that they afford a very insecure footing to a horse . . .*"

AT A GATE. "*Straight away go some at the nearest fence, others make for the gate in the corner of the field; and here the sportsman must beware of kicking horses and of being jammed against the gate-post. I give a little sketch of a small crowd at a gate. If the gate will not stay open but insists on swinging back heavily I would advise only strong men with their horses well in hand to struggle for the pleasure of showing the customary politeness to ladies. Crowded gateways are dangerous and are to be avoided, and much valuable time may be lost at them.*"

THROWN OUT. *"It is quite possible for experienced fox-hunters to lose the hounds during a run—to be 'thrown out,' as it is called, like our friend in the illustration—and to survey a vast tract of hill, dale, and wood without seeing a sign of the pack or the field."*

A SMALL FARMER. *". . . he may fall in with some dejected-looking 'small farmer' like the one I have drawn standing in the lane and have some deliberate conversation . . ."*

153

DON'T RIDE OVER THE SNOWDROPS. "*These are surely the 'brutal fox-hunters' of whom one reads, and they should be contrasted with that M.F.H. (by the way, he has since held the post of Master of the Horse), who, when his hounds were passing through a beautiful park in early spring, held up his hand to the field and called out, 'Gentlemen, pray don't ride over the snowdrops!' I give a drawing of the scene—it was in a park where those welcome little flowers grow in wild profusion under the naked beech trees.*"

PULLING DOWN A RAIL. *"And it is a great comfort as one grows in years and weight to be able to climb back easily to the saddle after dismounting to pull down a rail—like the gentleman in one of my illustrations—or to open an obstinate gate."*

OTHER WORKS

Caldecott is best remembered today for his illustrations for children. We tend to forget that his other work was exhibited in London galleries and brought him recognition as an artist. He exhibited at the Dudley Gallery, the Fine Art Society, the Grosvenor Gallery, the Institute of Painters in Water Colour, the Royal Academy, and the Royal Manchester Institution in Manchester.

Although he had exhibited at both the Royal Academy and Grosvenor Gallery in 1876, it was the exhibit of *The Three Huntsmen* in oil at the Royal Academy in 1878 which first brought serious attention to him as a painter.

The huntsmen were one of his favorite subjects. The bas relief, *Three Jovial Huntsmen,* cast in bronze in 1880, was probably executed after the oil painting. Caldecott used the same theme in his picture book *The Three Jovial Huntsmen* in 1880. However, he gave all three hunting horns and omitted the pack of hounds. The hunt changed from official form into a noisy chase across the countryside, setting a merry mood.

The Three Huntsmen

158

The morning walk, a wall panel

Two Swans. A decorative panel made for the dining room of the home of Henry Renshaw at Chapel-en-le-Frith near Macclesfield. Panel designed by W. E. Nesfield

159

Crouching Cat (about 1873 and 1874). Terra-cotta statuette
In February of 1873 Caldecott first started wax modeling for practice. In
August of the same year he was given a letter of introduction to the French
sculptor Dalou, who helped Caldecott develop his talent as a sculptor. The
Crouching Cat *provided Caldecott with a great understanding of the species,*
which he used in his illustrations of the cat in The Queen of Hearts *as well*
as this familiar cat from The House that Jack Built

Three Jovial Huntsmen, *bas relief, bronze*

John Gilpin's Ride. *A watercolor, bodycolor with pen and ink*
Probably painted after the success of the picture book, this illustration
shows Caldecott's talent as an artist

162

THE PICTURE BOOKS

Randolph Caldecott's *Picture Books,* originally published in sixteen parts by George Routledge and Sons of London, are the works for which he is remembered today. In December of 1978 *The House that Jack Built* and *The Diverting History of John Gilpin* will have the distinction of being continuously in print by various publishers for one hundred years.

From 1877 through 1885 Caldecott spent the spring and early part of the summer selecting the two rhymes to be illustrated. Caldecott not only provided the illustrations but designed the books and covers, including the advertisement which appeared on the back cover.

THE HOUSE THAT JACK BUILT

The House that Jack Built was the first of Randolph Caldecott's *Picture Books* and was published in time for the Christmas season of 1878. Brook House Farm, used as a model for *The House that Jack Built* by Caldecott, still stands at Hanmer, near Whitchurch. Shared happily with children by parents and teachers, this title remains one of the best loved of the sixteen books, since not only does it give pleasure, but it is a joyful introduction to the science of ecology.

It is interesting to note that the initials *E E* appear on several of the colored pictures. This shows that Edmund Evans personally engraved the wood blocks rather than give the task to one of the reproductive engravers in his employ.

"The Lightning Sketches" for *The House that Jack Built* remained unpublished until 1899, when they were printed for the benefit of London Hospital. They provide an interesting study of Caldecott at work.

Brook House Farm at Hanmer, near Whitchurch. Caldecott used it as a model for The House that Jack Built. *It can be recognized in spite of slight changes in the building*

This is the House that
Jack built

JACK
JO

Cat

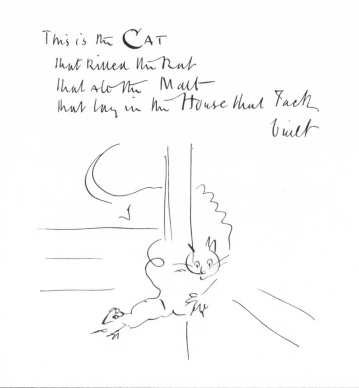

This is the CAT
that killed the Rat
that ate the Malt
that lay in the House that Jack
built

168

DOG

This is the DOG
that worried the Cat
that killed the Rat
that ate the malt
that lay in the House
that Jack built

169

This is the COW with the crumpled horn
that tossed the Dog
that worried the Cat
that killed the Rat
that ate the Malt
that lay in the House that
Jack built

COW

170

This is the MAIDEN all forlorn
That milked the Cow with the crumpled Horn
That tossed the Dog
That worried the Cat
That killed the Rat
That ate the Malt
That lay in the
House that Jack built

This is the MAN all tattered & torn
That kissed the Maiden all forlorn
That milked the Cow with the
crumpled Horn
That tossed the dog
That worried the Cat
That killed the Rat
That ate the malt
That lay in the House that Jack built

Maiden → MAN

171

This is the PRIEST all shaven Shorn

That married the Man all tattered Torn

That kissed the Maiden all ...

That milked the Cow ...

That ... the Dog

Jack built

This is the COCK ...

Jack built

Priest & Cock

172

This is the FARMer whosowed
the Corn

Farmer

173

THIS is the House that
Jack built.

3

This is the Malt,
That lay in the House that
Jack built.

This is the Rat,
That ate the Malt,
That lay in the House
that Jack built.

7

This is the Cat,

That killed the Rat,

That ate the Malt,

That lay in the House that Jack built.

This is the Dog,
That worried the Cat,
That killed the Rat,
That ate the Malt,
That lay in the House that
Jack built.

14

15

This is the Cow with the crumpled horn,

That tossed the Dog,

That worried the Cat,

That killed the Rat,

That ate the Malt,

That lay in the House that

Jack built.

19

This is the Maiden all forlorn,
That milked the Cow with the crumpled horn,
That tossed the Dog,
That worried the Cat,
That killed the Rat,
That ate the Malt,
That lay in the House
that Jack built.

This is the Man all tattered and torn,
That kissed the Maiden all forlorn,
That milked the Cow with
the crumpled horn,
That tossed the Dog,
That worried the Cat,
That killed the Rat,
That ate the Malt,
That lay in the House
that Jack built.

194

This is the Priest, all shaven and shorn,
That married the Man all tattered and torn,
That kissed the Maiden all forlorn,

That milked the Cow with
the crumpled horn,
That tossed the Dog,
That worried the Cat,
That killed the Rat,
That ate the Malt,
That lay in the House that
Jack built.

This is the Cock that crowed in the morn,
That waked the Priest all shaven and shorn,
That married the Man all tattered and torn,
That kissed the Maiden all forlorn,
That milked the Cow with
the crumpled horn,
That tossed the Dog,
That worried the Cat,
That killed the Rat,
That ate the Malt,
That lay in the House that
Jack built.

200

This is the Farmer who sowed the corn,

That fed the Cock that crowed in the morn,

That waked the Priest all shaven and shorn,

That married the Man all tattered and torn,

That kissed the Maiden all forlorn,

That milked the Cow with the crumpled horn,

That tossed the Dog,

That worried the Cat,

That killed the Rat,

That ate the Malt,

That lay in the House

that Jack built.

A study of the heads of rats which were used for The House that Jack Built

THE DIVERTING
HISTORY OF JOHN GILPIN

The Diverting History of John Gilpin was the second of Randolph Caldecott's *Picture Books* published in 1878 by George Routledge and Sons, London.

Caldecott was born on Bridge Street in the center of the busy old city of Chester. Certainly as a child he knew the noise and excitement of people coming to buy and sell their wares at the draper and mercer shops on Bridge Street. It is probable he had seen a horseman gallop through the busy crowded street and recalled the excitement of the scene when he decided to illustrate *John Gilpin*.

Cheapside, in London, with milling crowds and busy shops perhaps reminded him of the scenes of his childhood and thus he incorporated the tower of St. Mary-Le-Bow on that thoroughfare into his drawings.

Perhaps, also, he had seen a horseman scatter geese, for he certainly captured their spontaneous flight in the lively two-page picture so admired by Gauguin and Van Gogh when they examined Caldecott's drawings.

THE DIVERTING HISTORY

OF

JOHN GILPIN:

Showing how he went farther than he intended, and came safe home again.

WRITTEN BY Wm COWPER

WITH DRAWINGS BY R: CALDECOTT

JOHN GILPIN was a citizen
  Of credit and renown,
A train-band captain eke was he,
  Of famous London town.

John Gilpin's spouse said to her dear,
  " Though wedded we have been
These twice ten tedious years, yet we
  No holiday have seen.

" To-morrow is our wedding-day,
  And we will then repair
Unto the ' Bell ' at Edmonton,
  All in a chaise and pair.

" My sister, and my sister's child,
  Myself, and children three,
Will fill the chaise ; so you must ride
  On horseback after we."

The Linendraper bold

He soon replied, " I do admire
   Of womankind but one,
And you are she, my dearest dear,
   Therefore it shall be done.

" I am a linendraper bold,
   As all the world doth know,
And my good friend the calender
   Will lend his horse to go."

208

Quoth Mrs. Gilpin, "That's well said; And for that wine is dear, We will be furnished with our own, Which is both bright and clear."

John Gilpin kissed his loving wife; O'erjoyed was he to find, That though on pleasure she was bent, She had a frugal mind.

The morning came, the chaise was
   But yet was not allowed   [brought,
To drive up to the door, lest all
   Should say that she was proud.

So three doors off the chaise was stayed,
   Where they did all get in;
Six precious souls, and all agog
   To dash through thick and thin.

Smack went the whip, round went the
   Were never folks so glad!   [wheels,
The stones did rattle underneath,
   As if Cheapside were mad.

John Gilpin at his horse's side
   Seized fast the flowing mane,
And up he got, in haste to ride,
   But soon came down again;

For saddletree scarce reached had he,
   His journey to begin,
When, turning round his head, he saw
   Three customers come in.

So down he came; for loss of time,
   Although it grieved him sore,
Yet loss of pence, full well he knew,
   Would trouble him much more.

·The 3 Customers

211

'Twas long before the customers
    Were suited to their mind,
When Betty screaming came downstairs,
    "The wine is left behind!"

"Good lack!" quoth he, "yet bring it
    My leathern belt likewise,   [me,
In which I bear my trusty sword
    When I do exercise."

Now Mistress Gilpin (careful soul!)
    Had two stone bottles found,

To hold the liquor that she loved,
    And keep it safe and sound.

Each bottle had a curling ear,
    Through which the belt he drew,
And hung a bottle on each side,
    To make his balance true.

Then over all, that he might be
    Equipped from top to toe,
His long red cloak, well brushed and
    He manfully did throw.   [neat,

Now see him mounted once again
Upon his nimble steed,
Full slowly pacing o'er the stones,
With caution and good heed.

But finding soon a smoother road
Beneath his well-shod feet,
The snorting beast began to trot,
Which galled him in his seat.

"So, fair and softly!" John he cried,
 But John he cried in vain;
That trot became a gallop soon,
 In spite of curb and rein.

So stooping down, as needs he must
 Who cannot sit upright,
He grasped the mane with both his
 And eke with all his might. [hands,

His horse, who never in that sort
 Had handled been before,

What thing upon his back had got,
 Did wonder more and more.

Away went Gilpin, neck or nought;
 Away went hat and wig;
He little dreamt, when he set out,
 Of running such a rig.

The wind did blow, the cloak did fly
 Like streamer long and gay,
Till, loop and button failing both,
 At last it flew away.

Then might all people well discern
    The bottles he had slung;
A bottle swinging at each side,
    As hath been said or sung.

The dogs did bark, the children screamed,
    Up flew the windows all;
And every soul cried out, "Well done!"
    As loud as he could bawl.

Away went Gilpin—who but he?
    His fame soon spread around;
"He carries weight! he rides a race!
    'Tis for a thousand pound!"

And still as fast as he drew near,
    'Twas wonderful to view
How in a trice the turnpike-men
    Their gates wide open threw.

And now, as he went bowing down
  His reeking head full low,
The bottles twain behind his back
  Were shattered at a blow.

Down ran the wine into the road,
  Most piteous to be seen,
Which made the horse's flanks to
  As they had basted been. [smoke,

But still he seemed to carry weight.
With leathern girdle braced ;
For all might see the bottle-necks
Still dangling at his waist.

Thus all through merry Islington
These gambols he did play,
Until he came unto the Wash
Of Edmonton so gay;

And there he threw the wash about
    On both sides of the way,
Just like unto a trundling mop,
    Or a wild goose at play.

At Edmonton his loving wife
From the balcony spied
Her tender husband, wondering much
To see how he did ride.

"Stop, stop, John Gilpin!—Here's the
They all at once did cry; [house!"
"The dinner waits, and we are tired;"
Said Gilpin—"So am I!"

But yet his horse was not a whit
Inclined to tarry there;
For why?—his owner had a house
Full ten miles off, at Ware.

So like an arrow swift he flew,
Shot by an archer strong;
So did he fly—which brings me to
The middle of my song.

Away went Gilpin, out of breath,
  And sore against his will,
Till at his friend the calender's
  His horse at last stood still.

The calender, amazed to see
  His neighbour in such trim,
Laid down his pipe, flew to the gate,
  And thus accosted him:

"What news? what news? your tidings
  Tell me you must and shall— [tell;
Say why bareheaded you are come,
  Or why you come at all?"

Now Gilpin had a pleasant wit,
  And loved a timely joke;
And thus unto the calender
  In merry guise he spoke:

224

"I came because your horse would
    And, if I well forebode, [come :
My hat and wig will soon be here,
    They are upon the road."

The calender, right glad to find
    His friend in merry pin,
Returned him not a single word,
    But to the house went in ;

Whence straight he came with hat and
    A wig that flowed behind, [wig,
A hat not much the worse for wear,
    Each comely in its kind.

He held them up, and in his turn
    Thus showed his ready wit :
"My head is twice as big as yours,
    They therefore needs must fit."

"But let me scrape the dirt away,
    That hangs upon your face;
And stop and eat, for well you may
    Be in a hungry case."

Said John, "It is my wedding-day,
    And all the world would stare
If wife should dine at Edmonton,
    And I should dine at Ware."

So turning to his horse, he said
    "I am in haste to dine;

'Twas for your pleasure you came here,
    You shall go back for mine."

Ah! luckless speech, and bootless boast!
    For which he paid full dear;
For while he spake, a braying ass
    Did sing most loud and clear;

Whereat his horse did snort, as he
    Had heard a lion roar,
And galloped off with all his might,
    As he had done before.

226

Away went Gilpin, and away
    Went Gilpin's hat and wig;
He lost them sooner than at first,
    For why?—they were too big.

Now Mistress Gilpin, when she saw
    Her husband posting down
Into the country far away,
    She pulled out half-a-crown;

And thus unto the youth she said
    That drove them to the "Bell,"
"This shall be yours when you bring
    My husband safe and well." [back

The youth did ride, and soon did meet
    John coming back amain;
Whom in a trice he tried to stop,
    By catching at his rein.

But not performing what he meant,
    And gladly would have done,
The frighted steed he frighted more,
    And made him faster run.

Away went Gilpin, and away
Went postboy at his heels,
The postboy's horse right glad to miss
The lumbering of the wheels.

Six gentlemen upon the road,
Thus seeing Gilpin fly,
With postboy scampering in the rear,
They raised the hue and cry.

"Stop thief! stop thief! a highwayman!"
    Not one of them was mute;
And all and each that passed that way
    Did join in the pursuit

And now the turnpike-gates again
    Flew open in short space;
The toll-man thinking, as before,
    That Gilpin rode a race.

And so he did, and won **it too**,
    For he got first to town;
Nor stopped till where he had got up,
    He did again get down.

Now let us sing, Long live the King,
And Gilpin, long live he;
And when he next doth ride abroad,
May I be there to see.

The cover for The Milkmaid, *reduced from the original size*

THE MILKMAID

The Milkmaid has always been a personal favorite. One evening, assisting a four-year-old friend to bed, I was asked to share a story before putting out the lights.

"We will look at Shershey," I was told as the child headed toward a pile of well-worn books. I was delighted when "Shershey" turned out to be Caldecott's *The Milkmaid*.

"I know this. Why do you call it 'Shershey'?" I enquired.

"'Cause that's her name," came the prompt reply. I have always referred to the charming, independent young woman as "the milkmaid," so I suppose I looked puzzled. I was told impatiently, "It says so in the book. 'Nobody asked you Shershey said.'"

I thought I could hear Caldecott's ghost chuckling.

A

B

A) *This is the first rough sketch for the cover*

B) *This drawing for the cover shows the milkmaid as a more mature girl. Caldecott claimed the milkmaids in the dairy districts known to him did not marry when very young, which may be the reason he made the change*

C) *An early sketch of the opening page with text written in by Caldecott. When the final work was ready, he tightened the text as well as the drawings*

The MILKMAID,

An Old Song exhibited and explained in many designs by R. Caldecott.

A lady says to her son — a young Squire without much money — "You must seek a wife with a fortune".

C

The MILKMAID.

An Old Song exhibited & exhlained
in many designs by R. Caldecott.

═ A LADY said to her Son ─ a poor young SQUIRE:
"You must seek a Wife with a Fortune!"

244

"WHERE are you going, my Pretty Maid?"
"I'm going a-milking, Sir," she said.

"Shall I go with you, my Pretty Maid?"
"Oh yes, if you please, kind Sir," she said.

"What is your Father, my Pretty Maid?"

"My Father's a Farmer, Sir," she said.

"Shall I marry you, my Pretty Maid?"
"Oh thank you, kindly, Sir," she said.

"But what is your fortune, my pretty Maid?"
"My face is my fortune, Sir," she said.

"Then I can't marry you, my Pretty Maid!"
"Nobody asked you, Sir!" she said.

"Nobody asked you, Sir!" she said.

"Sir!" she said.

"Nobody asked you, Sir!" she said.

261

262

HEY DIDDLE DIDDLE

Hey Diddle Diddle and *Baby Bunting* were published in one volume by George Routledge and Sons, London, in 1882. This is a tremendous example of Caldecott's ability as an illustrator to develop the story beyond the brief text. The final drawing, filled with emotions, has never been suggested in the text. The deflated daughter-spoon accompanied by her angry father-knife and most dignified mother-fork are unforgettable.

On seeing these illustrations Kate Greenaway admitted her envy of Caldecott's talent as an illustrator. She, too, knew he stood alone as a leader in the field of illustrating for children.

Hey, diddle, diddle,

The Cat

and the Fiddle,

The Cow jumped over the Moon,

The little Dog laughed

to see such fun.

And the Dish ran away with the Spoon.

UNUSED DRAWINGS FROM
THE QUEEN OF HEARTS

The Queen of Hearts was published by George Routledge and Sons, London, 1881. These drawings were not used in the final book. Caldecott wrote his friend Frederick Locker-Lampson that at some time in the future he might expand the rhyme. It is possible the idea came to him when he made these sketches.

*This illustration appears
to be a rough sketch of
the Queen on the arm of
The Farmer's Boy, which
was published the same
year. Also published in
1881 was R. Caldecott's
Picture Book: Volume 2,
which was a reissue of
the second four of the
single books bound as
one. It would appear that
this rough sketch was
made while Caldecott was
preparing the cover
for that volume*

MISCELLANEOUS SELECTIONS FROM THE PICTURE BOOKS

Here are selected illustrations from *A Frog he would a-wooing go,* published in 1883 by George Routledge and Sons, London.

These drawings are included in this volume because they represent a new departure by Caldecott in illustrating for children. The verse is an old one. It probably originated as a spinning song, the words changing over the years.

A study of the drawings discloses the influence they bore on the work of Beatrix Potter, L. Leslie Brooke, and later illustrators.

At the time of their publication the reviewer for *The Nation* (December 13, 1883, New York) wrote that the colored drawings in Caldecott's newest work were "below his average" and "unworthy of the series." Today they are considered some of Caldecott's finest work.

Cover illustration for R. Caldecott's Second Collection of Pictures and Songs, *1885, George Routledge and Sons, London. This delightful garden party of the characters of the second eight of* the Picture Books *contained in this one volume is Caldecott at his best. Since Caldecott departed on his tour of the United States in late October 1885, it is doubtful he ever saw the printed cover*

LIST OF REFERENCES

BOOKS AND ARTICLES:

BLACKBURN, HENRY, *Randolph Caldecott: A Personal Memoir of His Early Art Career.* Sampson Low, Marston, Searle and Rivington, London, 1886.

BLISS, DOUGLAS PERCY, *A History of Wood Engraving.* J. M. Dent and Sons, Ltd., London; E. P. Dutton, New York, 1928.

CRANE, WALTER, *An Artist's Reminiscences.* The Macmillan Company, London, 1907.

CRANE, WALTER, *The Decorative Illustration of Books Old and New.* G. Bell and Sons, Ltd., London, 1896.

DARTON, F. J. HARVEY, *Children's Books in England, Five Centuries of Social Life,* 2nd ed. Cambridge University Press, London, 1958.

DAVIS, MARY GOULD, *Randolph Caldecott 1846–1886, An appreciation.* Lippincott, Philadelphia, 1946.

EVANS, EDMUND, *The Reminiscences of Edmund Evans,* edited by Ruari McLean. Oxford University Press, London, 1967.

KONODY, P. G., *The Art of Walter Crane.* George Bell and Sons, Ltd., London, 1902.

LAWS, FREDERICK, "Randolph Caldecott," *The Saturday Book,* Volume 16, pp. 61–83, London, 1956.

LINDER, LESLIE, *The Journal of Beatrix Potter.* Frederick Warne & Company, London and New York, 1966.

LOCKER-LAMPSON, FREDERICK, *My Confidences, An Autobiographical Sketch.* Charles Scribner's Sons, New York, 1896.

MAHONEY, BERTHA E., *et al.,* eds., *Illustrators of Children's Books, 1744–1945.* The Horn Book, Boston, 1947.

OVERTON, JACQUELINE, "Edmund Evans, Color-Printer Extraordinary," *The Horn Book Magazine,* Volume 22, pp. 109–18, Boston, 1946.

SMITH, IRENE, *A History of the Newbery and Caldecott Medals.* Viking, New York, 1957.

SPIELMAN, M. H., and LAYARD, G. S., *Kate Greenaway.* Adam and Charles Black, London, 1905.

TOWNSEND, JOHN ROW, *Written for Children: An Outline of English-Language Children's Literature.* Kestrel Books, London, 1974.

VAN STOCKUM, HILDA, "Caldecott's Pictures in Motion," *The Horn Book Magazine,* Volume 22, pp. 119–25, Boston, 1946.

NEWSPAPERS, MAGAZINES AND
PRIVATELY PUBLISHED BOOKLETS:

New York Daily Graphic, New York.
September 16, 1873, pp. 540, 542.
February 14, 1886, p. 7.
February 20, 1886, p. 780.

The New York Times, New York.
February 14, 1886, p. 7.

The Graphic, London.
   December 1876 through December 1887.

The Nation, New York.
   December 19, 1878, and December 18, 1879.

English Illustrated Magazine, London.
   1872 through 1886.

Harper's New Monthly Magazine, New York.
   No. CCLXXVII, June 1873, Vol. XLVII, pp. 67–86.

Illustrated London News, London.
   Vol. XXXIX, No. 1120, December 7, 1861, p. 578.

London Society, London.
   1871 and 1872.

Pictorial World, London.
   1872 through 1887.

Catalogue of a Loan Collection of the Works of Randolph Caldecott, exhibited at The Brasenose Club, Manchester, March 1888.

Rylands, Michael (Rector), *An Illustrated History of St. Oswald's, Malpas.* Cheshire, England, 1970.

COLLECTIONS EXAMINED:

The British Museum, Print Room, London.

The Caldecott Collection, The Caldecott Library, Whitchurch, Salop, England.

The Dr. Howard A. Kelly Caldecott Collection, St. Augustine Public Library, St. Augustine, Florida.

The Osborne Collection of Early Children's Books, Toronto Public Library, Toronto, Canada.

The Parker Collection, Houghton Library, Harvard University, Cambridge, Massachusetts.

St. Paul's Cathedral, London.

The Victoria and Albert Museum, Print Room, London, England.

The Chester Cathedral and Church School, Chester, Cheshire, England.

INDEX